I0620301

Siofra

The Sumaire Web, Volume 1

Anna Rose

Published by Sumaire Press, 2012.

This is a work of fiction. Similarities to real people, places, or events are entirely coincidental.

SIOFRA

First edition. January 30, 2012.

ISBN: 978-1393743095

Written by Anna Rose.

Also by Anna Rose

Tales of the Dragonguard
Aya's Dragon
Sara's Fire

The Sumaire Web
Siofra
Fiach Fola
Droch Fola

Watch for more at www.sumaire.com.

With Deepest Thanks

*L*et's face it. Books don't write themselves and trying to do everything yourself, from writing to research to editing really isn't particularly wise or even feasible. Having the best support system in the world makes all the difference. So...

Katherine, Tammy, CM, NJAM, LRB and Alice, you each helped make this book possible in your own way. Thank you for putting up with me during the course of writing this novel as I looked for inspiration. You all have graciously offered your beta'ing services, feedback and sometimes, just a big fat kick in the backside to get me writing again, at any hour of the day and night. You rock!

Author's Note

Readers beware. This isn't your standard modern vampire story.
I wanted to create something different from what is currently
being offered on the paranormal fiction market, as there seems to be an
awful lot of the same kind of stuff out there right now. When people
have heard that I am writing a vampire novel, it is obvious that they
envision impossibly beautiful, soulful monk-type male vampires and
the heaving bosoms of the human women who discover what they are
and fall madly in love with them. Thus, the next thing I find myself
doing is explaining that my writing and my protagonists are not like
that.

I like fully fleshed out characters that are more than
two-dimensional creations. My characters have lives (or unlives) during
which they have experienced love, hate, tragedy, sadness, happiness and
more. When you write the same characters long enough, they are going
to evolve, just as living real life people like you and me do. In the
best series, characters are not static. As they experience the fate their
creators put before them in each short story or novel in which they
appear, they learn and grow. Hopefully, this will make them into better
people and thus more interesting characters to follow.

So, if you are looking for doomed love, slobbering romance or
eternal teenagers in rut, you're not going to find it here. Not everyone
out there is trying to find a mate, nor are they necessarily looking to
be "saved" from their current existence. They may enjoy who and what
they are. Why would they want that to change?

As a bit of a heads up, the sun is not an issue for my vampires.
Like Bram Stoker's "Dracula", my vampires are able to walk in the
daylight. If you doubt me, read it sometime – and we are talking the

literary "Dracula", not the old 1930's theatrical version. Murnau's classic silent film, "Nosferatu" which starred German actor Max Schreck as the vampire Count Orlock, introduced the idea of sunlight destroying vampires.

Oh, and contrary to what you currently see on the small(ish) screen, no self-respecting vampire is going to stay in the same place for ten years straight, much less forty or fifty years, or even keep the same name through the years, unless they're a few pints short of a blood bank. The next time I hear or see that "guess I have good genes" excuse for looking perpetually young, I am going to scream.

Don't get me wrong. I do very much enjoy reading authors such as Laurell K Hamilton, Charlaine Harris, P.N. Elrod and the like. I enjoy their characters and the stories they tell. However, those are *their* stories, as mine are my own. We all have our own ideas about what we want to write and the characters we use to tell those stories. One thing we do seem to have in common is that we all appear to like to write strong female characters and do not have them swooning helplessly in a corner somewhere while their supernatural fanged hero comes along to rescue them.

In the end, I hope that you the reader will enjoy reading my stories as much as I have enjoyed writing them.

I do apologize for how long this "note" has become, but you may be able to tell that I feel strongly about the subject of vampires and the supernatural.

Chapter One

I held him close, looking for all the world like a mother...or even a lover. If it were not for certain rather glaringly obvious elements of this particularly touching scene, it might not generate further suspicion from passersby. Thus I was glad that this was a fairly well-abandoned area at this time of night. I absently stroked the man's back and rocked back and forth; his head still clutched close to my chest as I hummed tunelessly; a deranged lullaby to accompany the poor bastard into his terminal sleep.

My meal had been fairly light tonight, as he had already lost a considerable amount of blood by the time I found him. I had been drawn to him by the faint sound of his moans and the salty-sweet aroma of his blood that was carried on the faint breeze. His murderer was already long gone, which was a shame, as I could have feasted on that one without being self-conscious about it in the least. I certainly would not be spending these, his last few moments on the earthly plane, waiting until he passed beyond the Veil. What a shame, as I would have to settle for what was available.

These days, I do try to feed on the human stains of society as much as possible, but I have not always been so careful in my dining. There was a time when my choices were so limited that I was unable to pick and choose who would make my unfortunate acquaintance. Yes, my conscience would often prick me as I fed on a father, son, daughter or an innocent lover, after bringing him to the very height of excitement, when the heart pounds and blood rushes throughout the body in anticipation of the release to come.

As I am unable to be quite so carefree in this part of the world, my appetite is rarely sated, but I would like to think that I am cleaning up the streets a bit during those times when I take the worst of the city's criminals out of the picture.

It is very easy when first you wake to darkness, as it were, to loudly proclaim that you will only feed on the scum of the earth. High ideals and all that are supposed to make us better people. In practice, however, such nobility often finds itself being quietly swept under the rug as cruel necessity knocks us alongside our heads and points out that the grim reality of our existence is far harsher.

"Angels we may wish to be, but that we are actually demons is our only reality. To love a vampire is to love a predator. To love a human is to love your prey. Neither situation will end well when the hunger rises and one is left with no choice," I muttered the words under my breath. I had been taught that litany by a vampire I met during my time in Colonial-era though pre-revolutionary America. I had found it to be a painful truth.

Lub dub.

It was the hollow sound of the fluttering of his heart as it struggled to keep beating. One of the sounds that had alerted me to his presence in the first place, much as a hunting shark in the ocean is drawn to the splashing sounds of a wounded creature's distress. A symbol of how hard the human race has fought to survive against the bleakest adversity, even when so-called common sense might say that it is a completely lost cause. One cannot help but admire that kind of blind determination and stubborn tenacity.

But then, as has been said since even before I was an infant human child, beggars cannot be choosers; so there I was, feeding from some guy who smelled of clean skin, fresh clothes and some particularly nice smelling cologne that I am certain had not been cheap. This clearly was no child of the streets, and for some reason, his senseless death offended me, even if it did mean I would finally be able to feed.

It certainly was not like it had been in the old days, when, if one were financially fortunate, (or at an established and well run Haven), you could essentially visit the equivalent of a larder full of food, and safely close at hand, much like human farmers keep livestock. Those humans had grown accustomed to periodic "milking" as it were, in exchange for good treatment and in the case of modern Havens, a well-endowed retirement plan. Humans who served in Havens were often legacies, having been brought up in the culture, so they understood the need for complete discretion. They also knew the particularly draconian penalty for revealing secrets, so they were much less likely to blindly do so, as it not only affected them but any living ancestor or child of theirs.

If one were not quite so fortunate, you could hunt your prey as needed and then leave the remains for the local carnivores, carrion birds and insects. With few exceptions, that particular way of surviving was no longer open to the majority of vampires. Such was the case with being an Old World creature existing in modern times.

Lub dub.

Now, much of the world is not what it once was, and it is entirely too easy to be found out if you are not careful. Feeding has certain unchanging requirements and contrary to what one sees on television and in the movies, the advent of refrigeration has not been a particular boon for my kind. For example, blood needs to be consumed while still fresh and hot from a living human body. There are no other options. The common media conceit of blood stored in wine bottles in the refrigerator just is not possible, no matter how poetic and romantic it might appear to be.

Once it leaves its natural human container, the blood has already begun to putrefy, and is thus useless for me and my kind, and if you did not already know, blood bank bags contain an additive solution to retard clotting. It would indeed be nice to have that option, and when blood banks had first been created, many vampires had rushed to experiment, but very shortly thereafter found their bodies rather gruesomely rejecting what they had just ingested. Bagged blood might be perfect for sick humans in the hospital who are a pint or two low, but not for someone like me. You have to know something about vampire biology (or would that be necrology, as we're not actually alive?) to understand how awful it can be to ingest "dead", otherwise adulterated or even nonhuman blood. You would actually have to be fairly desperate or deranged even to contemplate drinking nonhuman blood, as animals do not register as a food source to vampiric senses.

It really is quite surprising that vampires have remained hidden for this long. Yes, we do occasionally make human connections and the very rare friendship, but those are scarce as hen's teeth. I haven't had a human I could truly call "friend" in perhaps the last hundred years, and the sum total I could boast for my entire existence as a vampire could be counted on the fingers of one hand with some left over for rude gestures. Vampire friendships are more actions of necessity, and tend to be more strong acquaintance than anything else. Yes, we do share a common condition, but vampires tend instinctively to be fairly selfish creatures where other vampires are concerned and seem to stay in close quarters only as long as is absolutely necessary. One such situation is when a vampire has brought a mortal over and that Maker keeps their Child under their guidance and protection. In this relationship, the young one learns about what they are and the blessings and limitations it places upon them in a relatively safe atmosphere. Finally, some long-term vampire partnerships that border on marriage do thrive, but I know of only two that still exist.

Lub dub.

As it is, the majority of my kind by necessity has become solitary and far-flung in an effort to avoid overtaxing a particular area. In the unlikely event that we meet another of our kind, we are careful to ask permission to hunt, if we are in a position where we have no choice, as long-standing vampire custom of the past one hundred fifty years or so allows one vampire to kill another who poaches. Once in a very great while, if and when one of my kind becomes thoughtless in their actions, one or two of us will come together to bring an end to the wildling before causing irreparable harm. I had participated in two such adventures over the centuries. It is not something that is at all easy to do. You are still ending someone; even though it is ultimately for the greater good and the safety of all, both vampire and human. Think of Jack the Ripper.

Yes, him.

The cutting was all about misdirection on his part, but he was attracting far too much attention. Thus, the greater vampire community had been forced to come together in order to permanently resolve the situation.

You might be interested to know that contrary to popular belief, "Jack" was not a royal. Well, at least, not a contemporary one for the time. Moreover, I am not going to tell you to which royal House he belonged. I doubt you would recognize the name, anyway.

Lub dub.

I do not often do any real hunting anymore, having become more of a scavenger in a part of the world that has grown much too scientifically and forensically sophisticated for me to be careless. Thus, I have learned to avoid leaving evidence of my existence. I am not always successful, and that has sometimes led to some rather interesting sounding cold cases, but that has always been the exception, rather than the rule.

This time, after using the remains of his shirt to carefully brush away as much gun powder residue from the area as I could (for the record, cordite tastes like crap), I placed my mouth over the puncture wound. The man's thoracic artery, damaged in the attack, was leaking large amounts of blood, so it was the natural place for me to feed. I angled his body so the wound was lower than his legs, then sucked gently to avoid damaging the skin any more than was necessary, using gravity as much as possible to ease the flow of his blood. Though it was not much, even with the use of simple physics, I eagerly swallowed what bubbled forth, being very careful not to allow my fangs to tear his skin.

He was too far gone for me to have bothered to get him any medical attention, the congealing blood that lined the gutter for several dozen feet before pouring into a storm drain mute witness to the futility of any such attempt. I could hear the sound of vermin approaching, already attracted to the scene by the scent of all that exposed and now wasted blood. To the rodents and the feral cats and dogs in the area, I just smelled like another predator, certainly not human, so beyond a natural wariness on their part, my presence would not be enough to keep them away. Humans, they seem to have learned, would try to kill them, whereas another predator would be more interested in defending its share of the bounty so near to hand. but would not necessarily attempt to kill any challenges.

Once I had drunk all that I was able without resorting to obviously damaging the body, I was as you found me at the start of this narrative, cradling the man in my arms and watching over him as his heart made its final weak thumps and then subsided into the inevitability of his own death. He had lost consciousness sometime before I found him, so he might not even have known that someone was with him as he passed from this world into the next, but I could not justify leaving him before I knew him to be completely gone. When the time came where everything that made this man the person he had been was gone, and the body nothing more than a lump of decomposing flesh, I could leave it to the elements and those who were still able to make use of what remained.

Lub...dub.

His heartbeat was becoming weaker, and I knew there was but little time left for him on this earth. He should have died already from blood loss, but for some reason, he hung onto whatever remained of his life as tenaciously as a Jack Russell terrier does a rat. Was his mind already gone from lack of oxygen? Was his spirit floating overhead, watching all that transpired below him, and waiting for that fabled White Light to appear to guide him on his way? I surely was not in any position to know.

I could see from looking at the exposed skin on his arms that life had not been easy for him, for one reason or another. The scars of countless needle punctures marred the inside of his elbow and he had not been too healthy before the shooting that had ultimately ended his life. Fortunately, my own condition kept me safe from anything he might have harbored, as there was not a living thing within me to nourish or otherwise nurture the vile microbes that currently plagued the human race. I had tasted disease in his blood, not drug abuse, so the old needle marks were probably from whatever diagnosis and treatment he had gotten for it. Perhaps that strength and tenacity that kept him alive now was what had helped him survive his illness, though I could taste that his illness was still in the process of killing him.

I could feel my body responding to what little moisture it had been able to absorb, so I knew there was a better chance that I could pass in human company without garnering unwanted attention. The longer I had gone without giving in to my growing hunger, the more my flesh had begun to dehydrate; however, I was currently in a place where random hunting and feeding was not at all a safe thing to do. Thus, I had had to conceal myself from human eyes for the past week or so, as my skin had begun to draw tightly over the bones of my face, giving it a skull-like appearance. To be honest, my most recent feeding would not make me appear hale and hearty, but I certainly had less of a chance of frightening innocent passersby. Those to whom I was to speak were lead to believe that I was seriously ill. It just does not do to tell them "why, I'm a starving vampire!" when one's health is asked after. People tend to rush away all wild-eyed, believing you are a dangerous lunatic.

Lub dub.

Two weeks was really entirely too long for a vampire to go without feeding if one wanted to continue to blend in, and I knew it was time to find another place, preferably a less technologically blessed location than North America. Maybe even one of the more violent countries in the world, where sudden death was far more common for a larger portion of the population and disappearances elicited little curiosity overall beyond immediate family members. In fact, I preferred quieter world locations.

I mean, who would not? However, probably since the time of the first vampire, my kind have always had a much easier time surviving during periods of violent civil disturbance. Vampires still tend to gather in larger concentrations in places like the Middle East, where violence, sadly, seems to be a part of daily life. Peace has a habit of leading to famine, in my not inconsequential lifetime. I do appreciate and certainly understand the blessings it brings; however, vampires tend to do poorly when it occurs.

"Kathy..." the first thing I had heard him say since I arrived, a whisper so soft only I could hear him. His face screwed up in a kind of pain I truly think had nothing to do with his injuries or the results of my feeding. I saw sadness and regret so raw that I could almost feel it, myself. I leaned in closer, in case he had something else to say, but my over four centuries of experience told me that I would be disappointed.

"Rest, child. Your reward is waiting for you," I told him, not knowing if he could even hear me. Although he technically was older than I was, as he seemed about thirty mortal years old to my eternal nineteen, anyone currently living would forever be a child to me. "Your Kathy wouldn't want you to suffer, lad."

Lub...dub

Perhaps he had heard me, after all and maybe I had been able to give him a measure of peace at the last, because I saw a satisfied smile flirt across his face. I could feel his blood, what there was of it, seeping toward the most dehydrated parts of my body and felt gratitude for what he had given me because of his impending death.

"Thank you," I murmured to him.

He had an interesting face, with features that, if taken alone, were not particularly attractive, but put them together and it made for a beautiful face. I could see the crinkle of laugh lines at the corners of his eyes, how the edges of his mouth curved upward in the suggestion of a smile. Even as death approached, good-natured mischief constantly showed within his expression. Unconsciously, I smiled back at him, though I knew his eyes were shut and he was unable to see me.

I slowly ran my hand down the slowly cooling flesh of his strong jawline, feeling the almost invisible stubble that was there, my thumb coming to rest on the indentation on his chin. The cleft was not as strong as the one on a particularly popular mid to late twentieth century movie actor, but close enough for government work. This had been someone who caught the eye when he passed by.

Despite his illness, this human had been well fed and showed none of the signs of exposure that so many of the homeless seemed to display. A cursory examination of his teeth revealed all his natural teeth still resident and in excellent condition, with only a filling or two to indicate regular dental care. There was every chance that someone would end up missing him in very short order. Perhaps that someone would be this "Kathy" person to whom he had called out with one of his very last breaths.

Lub...dub

Not for the first time during moments such as this, I wondered if his parents were still alive, if he were married, if he had kids. It is not as though I am the vampire version of the hooker with a heart of gold, famous in myth, song and other media. I have to feed and have no desire to embrace the true death, so ending myself just is not in the cards. I can and do wonder, though, about those upon whom I feed. Were they someone who had already or might one day have made great discoveries or someone who would bring into the world someone who would accomplish great deeds...and did that really matter now? What

13

is done is done, and you cannot change the past, as much as you might like to do just that.

"Who are you and why were you in this alley?" I asked him. "What was so important that you went to the dangerous part of town and got yourself killed? Will your family miss you? Do they know where you've gone?"

It has been so long now that I can barely remember my own family. Yes, there are tiny bits and pieces of my childhood that will dance across the surface of my memory, but not unlike the will o' the wisp, they are nearly impossible to grab hold of to examine more closely. They are like snapshots in a photo album full of random photographs: moments caught without real context or framing. I remember more of the few years before I was turned than I do my childhood. Of course, part of the reason for that was because of the disputes between Roman Catholic Ireland and Anglican Catholic England.

The lives of many of the people around me ultimately seem to be as fleeting as the life expectancy of a piece of flash paper to which a match has been applied. I do not dare get too attached to any of them, as it hurts too much to watch them age and die, while I stay the same as I have been for the past several hundred years, except that now I am one of the palest Irish women you will probably ever see.

Lub...

Chapter Two

I was born sometime around the year 1620, but I do not have a specific date. I believe I was somewhere around thirteen years old at the time. I grew up somewhere east of Iveragh, near the eastern shore of Ireland. Keep in mind that I only have recorded history to use as a timeline. They were, as the Chinese have long reckoned such things, "interesting times", so at least I have something to use as a rude measure of sorts. By the way, that phrase does not mean anything good, but instead reminds one that things that are "interesting" enough to hit the history books generally involve bad situations. Why else would they be interesting to others?

I know that I was turned sometime just before the Irish Rebellion of 1641, when the good Roman Catholics of Ireland tried once again to wrest control of our country from the Protestant English. Even in the twenty first century, things are still tense between certain groups of people. Ah, religion has played a big hand in the shaping of our world, has it not?

I remember the nickname my mother gave me, Siofra, rather than my birth name. Siofra is the Gaelic for "elf". In my mother's case, it was, perhaps, a reference to my frequently unladylike childhood antics and mischief. Perhaps she considered me a changeling, but at this late date, I will never know.

"Siofra! Get yourself down from that boulder, grab this crock and go help your brother with the milking!" was a common refrain in the evenings while I was growing up. It was not that I deliberately shirked my chores, more that I loved watching the sun as it began to set and changed the colors in the sky. I knew from stories my mother had told me that there were people who actually painted beautiful representations of both sunrises and sunsets, but had never seen such artwork, myself.

My current surname, Bothran, is a veiled reference to my favorite instrument, the bodhrán, a kind of drum. At this point in time, I do not clearly remember the surname with which I was born, but it seems as though Ó Sé would be close. Even with that vague information, however, I would not be so stupid as to keep exactly the same name through the centuries. I generally change it every decade or two. Of course, these days, I never stay in one location for longer than a decade or so before moving on.

When I was a child, there was no such thing as an idyllic childhood for someone from my station in life. There were no nurses, no governesses, and no afternoon tea. You had two meals a day if you were lucky, but oftentimes you only had a morning meal and would eat again the next morning.

Children were expected to work from an early age, helping to support themselves and the entire family, and complaining about it would never have been tolerated. I think it might even have been unthinkable, unlike with the whiny, lazy kids of today who cannot be bothered to clean their rooms without drama and angst, much less pick rock and weeds from a field full of turnips and cabbages. When I was about three years old, I put to work picking rock out of my mother's kitchen garden, as it was easy to discern a rock from something edible easily, even to a relative toddler.

I still chuckle a bit knowing that gardens do indeed sometimes seem to grow rocks in addition to actual food. It never seemed as though we managed to pick all the rocks out of the kitchen garden or the field. There were always more to throw onto the pile. One day, you would have spent the hours between dawn and dusk moving inconvenient rocks from the field to the stone pile and the next morning, you would come back to the field to discover more had apparently magically sprouted overnight. Father was convinced that the Fae were behind it, but try as he might, he was never able to catch them at their mischief.

I do recall that when my chores for the day were finished, I could often be found in the branches of the tallest oak tree near our family's farmhouse, an old building constructed of stone with a thatch roof. I would clamber up into its welcoming branches at every opportunity, gathering acorns while I was up there, tucking them into the deep pockets of my apron, so often mended that it was more patch than apron, for safety. Coming home with an apron full of acorns, or if the season was right, a double handful of elderberries, would often keep my mother from beating me quite so harshly for my tomboyish antics.

My parents had been Irish peasants who worked a few acres of land for a great lord, in exchange for a portion of the harvest and I was the pre-teen daughter who was sold off to that lord after a hard year that had yielded poor crops. Rents were owed and there was no money and no produce to pay those rents, so I became the payment. My family did not own the land, but my father had no skills that would have made him valuable in a village, so he was forced to make his own living any way he could. His own father had tilled this same land in his day, so my father took up his own plow, rake and hoe and did the same when his father became too old to do it himself.

My paternal Grandfather and Grandmother were buried on a corner of the acreage in a plot surrounded by some of the very same stones that had been plucked from the fields over the years. I still remember that my Grandfather would dandle me on his knee and sing bright cheerful songs in my ear. He had died suddenly one day, not too long after my Grandmother passed. It was as though the life had gone out of him when she died and he lost his will to live without her any longer. I believe that theirs was a love match, rather than something that had been arranged between their parents, and while they were alive, things were happier in my whole family. Some of that love I felt for him is still inside me, though I keep it bottled up tightly.

I remember having at least one brother, if not two. I remember hearing the name Sean or Shane, but I am not sure which. I do not believe that those were the names of two boys, which would mean that if I did have a second brother, I have no clue what he would have been called.

Sons who could assist their father in tilling the land were far more important to a peasant family than a mere female child who must be closely monitored to be sure she remained chaste until a suitable marriage contract could be arranged. There were far too many daughters amongst the peasant families on the lands surrounding our allotment, so making such an arrangement, as poor as my family was, was very unlikely. At my age, I was more a burden than a blessing, so I know he deeply resented my remaining at his table as just another mouth to feed.

"Send her to the Abbess," he even suggested one night when the table had been nearly bare for the fourth time in a week. When I was turned away at the gate because the Abbess required payment to take me into the convent, I had been bundled back home. That was when my sleeping arrangements had changed to the point that I slept with the dogs.

My father had refused to part with anything he truly valued when the steward showed up to collect the delinquent annual rents, instead offering me up as a drudge for the lord's house. I am certain that he saw this as some Divinely granted opportunity to be rid of me. The last memory I have of my parents is Mam's face streaked with tears as I was torn from her grasp by my father and very nearly flung over the horse's backside like a sack of potatoes. As the steward yanked his nag's head around to return to the lord's manse, I saw my Da give me a piercing, unfriendly look, and then turn away to tend to his rusting scythe. Apparently, my leaving was inconveniencing him and I remember having the fleeting impression that somehow, he saw all of this as being my fault, which was odd as he did not want me around anyway.

Once we were out of sight of my family's small farm, the steward, whom I later learned was called Seth, stopped his horse and rather surprisingly to me, gently pulled me up to ride pillion behind him. To my profound embarrassment, my stomach ventured an opinion of its currently empty state and broke the uneasy silence, to which the steward raised a questioning eyebrow.

The man said not a word, continuing to adjust his and my seats until I straddled the horse's posterior in a much less precarious fashion. He directed me to grab hold of his belt and hook my fingers into it from the top. It gave me a much better sense of balance, so I did not argue.

Once he knew I was secure in my seat, he reached into his leather purse and pulled out a ragged cloth which, when untied, revealed a hunk of hard dark bread. He broke the compact but very dense travel loaf into two pieces of a reasonably equal size and then handed some to me, before clucking to his horse and continuing our journey at an easy walk. He had been kind enough to be sure I sat atop the bit of horse blanket which protruded from beneath the saddle, so my own rear end was saved from painful congress with the horse's bony spine.

Being no fool and wanting to prevent further gastronomic conversation, I jammed the bread into my mouth and let my saliva moisten it a bit before I was finally able to choke it down with a mouthful of watered wine from his battered but still quite serviceable wineskin. Food was food, and to waste it was insult to, if not the gods themselves, the cook who had prepared it. I had learned to eat food that was barely this side of edible during the past couple seasons, as the best was generally saved for my father and brothers, who did the majority of the heavy work on our small holding. These meager offerings were magnificent, compared to some meals I had been forced to eat or starve for stubbornness. The bread was followed by a small piece of dried meat and another swallow from the skin.

There are times that I think I can recall what regular human food tastes like, but then I realize that so much time has gone by that I could not possibly remember that far back. I seem to recall that that small bit of dark bread tasted like heaven itself to tastebuds accustomed to even plainer fare. The dried meat itself was a treat, as it had been soaked in a wonderfully salty brine solution before being set out to dry in the heat of the day. I remember teasing out every last bit of salt I could from its fibers before I finally swallowed it. I know that the scent of cooked human food makes my stomach turn a bit now that I am a vampire, and so I avoid being near it if I can at all manage that. That said, I do know that while I was still living, I certainly enjoyed it and that I had a particular fondness for the flavor and texture of meat, beef in particular, though I ate that rarely.

"You seem a strong girl. No tears from you, I see," Seth commented almost conversationally as we rode, reaching back and patting my leg with an encouraging tone in his voice. "I am sure a place can be found for you at the manse. I can promise you a full stomach every day and your own pallet on which to sleep."

I know now that he was trying to be kind and set my heart at ease, but at the time, all I knew was that I was being ripped from the only life I had known and pressed into a life of service with only strangers to keep me company. Sheer stubbornness on my part kept me from dissolving in tears at all of this. I was not going to show fear in front of a stranger.

"I am not afraid of anything," I lied, as much to myself as to him. I am sure he knew it was a falsehood, but he did not remark on it, instead we rode the rest of the way in an uneasy silence.

Once at the manse, I do not recall ever being called by name by anyone other than the steward, and even that was my nickname.

Perhaps it was part of the process of completely separating me emotionally from my family and tying me to my new home and master.

I remember being called by epithets both crude and passing polite; however, I was a non-entity, little more than a drudge. Unless one was family, one did not normally have close relationships in that household. I am sure that Seth knew my given name. I know that because he kept the household records, but even he generally called me "girl" or "child". He had introduced me to the other servants by name, but they, too, all quickly fell to using diminutives and easy nicknames when dealing with me. I suppose it was easier for them to do so.

I spent most of my days scrubbing out whatever happened to need cleaning at any given time. The one time I had been foolish enough to let myself be seen in the hall by the mistress of the manse, I had been beaten so badly that I could not rise from my pallet in the stable for a few days. After that great mistake on my part, I remained below stairs as much as possible and kept to the shadows, learning to hide myself quickly whenever I heard voices or footsteps nearby.

In those days, you grew up young or you would end up dying young. This was true for all layers of a society that betrothed infants and married daughters off shortly after they had their first period. Childhood was not really "invented" until the late latter half of the 19th century in the United States. I was not from the class where infant betrothal would be an issue; however, once I physically became a woman, there was every chance I would be married off to one of the other household servants and any children I might bear as a result becoming yet another commodity for the lord of the house.

Marrying for love was something else that really had not been invented yet, not that I was swooning over anyone on the master's grounds or that any of them was courting me. Of course, I was not doing anything to make myself more attractive, either. I had one ragged gown that I wore all the time, even while sleeping, and at the time, bathing was a suspect thing. Therefore, beyond periodically washing my face and pulling a comb through the knots in my hair and then once again tying it into a rude bun at the back of my head, there was not much to recommend me. One of the stable boys had once attempted to rape me, but a swift knee to his nether regions quickly distracted him from his original purpose, and from that time on, I did my best to avoid being alone with him.

It was as the steward had promised. I never hungered for long, as the kitchen always seemed to present more food than even the fat lord, his vast family and sycophants could ingest in one sitting. Perhaps the steward had said something to the cook about my embarrassingly talkative stomach, but I never dared to ask. Mistress Fairworth, the cook, who called me *"Dearg"* (Irish Gaelic for "red") for the brassy splash of color on my head, constantly kept an enormous kettle of meat and vegetable porridge on a hook at the outside edge of the kitchen fire, to which she would add each day's leftovers and then more water to keep it wet. There were probably parts of that porridge that were at least a decade old, I am certain. I had a large wooden bowlful twice a day, eating it with bread culled from the day's baking. It did not take me long to discover that Mistress Fairworth prided herself on the tasty comestibles she was able to provide not only to the lord and his family, but to all others who fed from her deep ladle. Indeed, children and nursing mothers thrived on what she provided them. Many households subsisted on what little meat they could get and coarse bread, but Mistress Fairworth somehow knew that vegetables were an important part of a healthy diet.

"People in my care usually keep their teeth well into their twenties," she would boast to anyone who would listen. I do not know if she was aware of scurvy and that it could lead to tooth loss, but her foresight was a boon to those for whom she cooked. I have no idea how she could have come by that information, as she was a landlubber, born on the property on which we all lived, and never more than five miles away from it.

SIOFRA

It was common during that time in history for people to lose several teeth in one way or another by the time they reached their mid-twenties, but that was not the case here under the care of Mistress Fairworth. I was lucky to grow up with her feeding me, and to learn how to continue to feed myself later on, because I had a mouthful of very strong and healthy teeth by the time I met my untimely end. I am also sure that her teaching me to clean my teeth at least once daily with the frayed end of a twig did not hurt, either. I know my breath certainly stunk less than many of my peers'.

When I had arrived at the manse, Mistress Fairworth had taken one look at me and clucked her tongue in dismay. She then set one of the fat old kitchen gardeners to combing the lice from my hair using an old fine-toothed bone comb she produced from out of her big wooden chest, and then popping the nits between her fingernails after having me stripped bare and then immersing me for a good scrubbing in one of the horse troughs. The ragged shift and apron in which I had arrived was unceremoniously thrown on the midden fire without a second glance. Its successor was the rough spun and very itchy brown woolen gown I now wore, which had been unearthed from one of the storage trunks the cook kept in some back room of the kitchen area. I was permitted to leave her sight with an injunction to be careful with it, as I would not receive another for at least a year's time.

Daily, I broke my fast just after the big black and red cock who ruled the kitchen yard crowed in the approach of the morning sun. The sun's colorful fingers would just be beginning to reach up into the sky in order to haul itself overhead for the day at that time, and it was a beautiful thing to watch from the vantage of the kitchen stoop. Much later in the day, I would take my supper before I had my turn at scrubbing the evening meal's pans and platters, thereafter retiring for the night. Wisely, Mistress Fairworth had the servants' meals scheduled out over the course of the day, so that she would not be overrun with nimble fingers attached to greedy stomachs and perhaps experience thievery of more choice bits of food while she was distracted doling out ladlesful of thick porridge as her thick-witted and wall-eyed daughter Meg handed out the bread. I considered myself lucky indeed that I could break my fast so shortly after I awoke, after having brought in the night's eggs from the ever-obliging hens that the cock serviced so expertly.

Those who tended the manse while the rest of the house slept had their meals brought to them in a communal bucket in the middle of the night by the cook's night assistant, who was simply called Frost. He would wait quietly as they gobbled their food, and then take the empty bucket back to the kitchen, scraped nearly clean by nimble fingers and stale bread crusts.

Frost was an oddly pale man with very light eyes, an acne-scarred face and a marked limp. He was the one who set the dough to rising for the day's bread before retiring to his pallet at the back of the pantry for the day. On those rare occasions that we encountered one another while both of us were up and about; he would glance at me and give a short nod and a grunt before continuing onto whatever errand he might be about at that moment. During my first few years at my new home, I do not believe we exchanged a single word between us.

I cannot say that I truly liked the man, but I had a reasonably comfortable familiarity with him that made him much less threatening than he might be to a young girl such as me. He offered me no harm, and I returned that favor in word and deed. Some of the kitchen staff would whisper about him when they thought no one else was listening, with some saying that his scarred face was the result of a deal with the Devil or some such nonsense, and others saying that he limped because one of his legs was hoofed. Of course, I believed none of that.

My pallet, which was in a corner of the stable's hayloft, was indeed my own. When I was still living with my parents, once I reached a certain age, I was bundled off to the corner of the house where my mother cooked our meals, to share a rude pallet with the flea and louse-infested hounds and the one cat my father allowed us to keep as a mouser and ratter. My father, mother and brothers shared the wide bed between them, even when my father took his nightly husbandly rights to screw my mother and maybe knock her around a bit. I would close my eyes tightly and shove my fingers deep into my ears to try to keep from hearing what was going on so close to where I lay. I was fortunate that I did not now have to share the loft space in my new situation with anyone else, though I had found a safe place up there to squirrel away any valuables I might collect along the way.

I built some alliances early on, in order to stay as safe as I could. Being completely on one's own was never safe. Allies, be they made by love or necessity, could help keep you alive at that time in history. Both Seth and Mistress Fairworth were my two human allies, but the nonhuman one I carefully cultivated was one of the most important of my young life, if not my first several decades on this planet.

One of the yard's five guard dogs, a Wolfhound who was perhaps six months or so old, had taken a shine to me (the twice-daily leavings from my big wooden bowl sweetening the relationship, I am certain), shortly after I had been attacked by the stable boy. As with all dogs, he was looking for as close to an "alpha" position as he could find, but the other four dogs had better relationships with the Houndsman, so when I extended the hand of friendship to the massive dog, he was quick to seize the opportunity. At first, because Irish Wolfhounds were incredibly valuable and prized as the companions of the nobility, the Houndsman had tried keeping him from me. Several escapes later on the part of the dog, and the man finally threw up his hands in defeat. I do not know what the man told our master, but I was never punished for having the dog's friendship.

Of course, the dog was quick to keep the grounds safe, but when I was available and approachable, he never left my side.

Thus, each evening, before I went for my supper, I would give the dog the leavings from that morning, and the next morning, he would get my supper leavings, thus he appeared to make a point of sleeping at the foot of the ladder to the loft, in case he missed the food I had caused him to expect from me. I would slip him the occasional leftover bone from the kitchen as well, to which he always responded with a toothy grin and tail wagging. When he was unable to guard them himself, he would hide his prizes in random places, but he always seemed to be able to find what he had stashed away.

My largess ensured that the massive dog was always nearby and attentive. His given name was Titus, but my secret name for him was *Mathúin,* which is the Gaelic for "bear". I would hear him growl sometimes at night, when I was about to go to sleep, and once or twice, I heard the sound of someone running away as Mathúin's growl become a bloodcurdling roar and he raced out after whomever had tried to slip by him. At least once, I heard a shriek of pain and shortly thereafter, Mathúin would trot back in and flop back down in his accustomed place to doze lightly.

Instead of frightening me, it made me feel protected and safe, and I would roll over and slip into sleep, knowing that Mathúin was watching over me. In the morning, once he finished the remains of last night's supper, he would walk with me to the trough, where I would wash out my bowl before entering the kitchen to break my fast for the day. He had learned that sometimes I might give him the odd chunk of meat from my bowl while it was still warm, instead of making him wait all day long, along with a good scratch, before I officially started my own day.

My days and nights continued with little variation, except that as I got older and showed myself capable, Mistress Fairworth set me to positions that were more responsible. I will be the first to admit that I did not miss scrubbing pots or picking rock and weeds. Such chores were given to those who had shown no talent for much of anything else. I was able to tend a stewpot or a spit without letting things burn, and had a decent hand for mending and embroidery, when necessary, so I ended up working inside the manse, rather than outside.

"You are a dab hand at embroidering the ladies' kerchiefs, Dearg," she told me more than once as I sat at her broad kitchen table. Mathúin would doze contentedly at my feet as I carefully decorated the lacy wisps of cloth that the manse's noble ladies often carried to dab at their eyes and noses or to conceal sachets of pleasant smelling dried flowers and herbs. "I wish I had that gift, myself."

She would prattle on about this or that during those times, keeping busy by tidying her kitchen to her satisfaction or sometimes even sitting for a little while as we shared a bit of tea and Mathúin gnawed on a stale loaf of dark bread which had been soaked in tasty pot liquor. I knew I was lucky and did my best not to jeopardize my good fortune. I always found it to be curious that Mistress Fairworth did not show this kind of attention to her own Meg, but then that one was seventeen, already married and living with her husband, Gibbon, who tended the goats. Their own living quarters took up a single small room off the stable.

Life was not easy as a servant, but it was not impossible, either. We were blessed enough to have a reasonably generous lord who did not scrimp on food when it came to those who worked for him. Servants in other houses often did with little more than a crust of bread and weak ale to sustain them from one day to the next. Such was often the lot of those who served. Many lords seemed to feel that as they already provided shelter and an honest living for those who eased their own lives, that little else was required in the way of board.

I had seen some of these unfortunates when they visited in the company of their own masters and mistresses. Clucking disdainfully at their sharp features caused by lack of body fat, and in many cases infirm from long-term malnutrition, our Cook often took it upon herself to try to put a little more meat on their bones by slipping them an extra meat roll or ladleful of stew while they were in her demesnes. I knew that the results of her efforts would be short-term at best, but I know it had to have been nice to have a belly full of something more than stale bread. When she could, she would even contrive to give them a hunk of whatever cheese she had at hand, along with some dried meat, popped into their bag by one of the more nimble and sneaky children of the house as they departed.

If our lord had ever discovered her actions, she likely would have suffered a terrible beating; however, the rest of the servants looked after her as she looked after them. In my time on the premises, one or two taken beatings that should by rights have gone to her, when they claimed they had been the ones to give the foodstuff to the unsuspecting visiting servant. After those beatings, Mistress Fairworth had taken special care of those martyrs to the delicacies of her kitchen.

There came a time when I would substitute for Frost when he was taken ill or had been sent on some errand that took him away from the house. He was not a young man, thus there were times when the common afflictions of old age made a higher claim on his abilities than he was able to counter in order to perform his duties. He was quite fortunate that this lord allowed those who had outlived their usefulness to remain on the premises. Many would have turned them out to die, once they were unable to perform.

Maybe some three years following my arrival in the lord's kitchen, Seth, the steward, came to me with his eyes downcast and his hat in his hands. He bore the sad news of the passing of my family by some sort of plague.

"As I do every year about this time, I went to collect the rents. I hailed the house several times, but heard no sound from them. It was then I saw the milch goat dead on the stoop. Tied out as it was, it had eaten and drunk all it could reach."

"My family is dead? All of them? Dead?" I cried out. "How can you be sure?"

"I took a very long fallen branch from the great tree and pushed the door open. The smell from the inside of the house was something out of

Hell, itself. I'm so very sorry, lass." It seemed he could not bring himself to look at me. For some reason, he seemed to feel a sense of guilt. "I did not dare go closer. I did not want to bring plague here to the rest of us."

I curtly thanked him for his news, and then ran out the door and climbed up into my hayloft, where I digested the tragic news I had received. What could have gone through the family so quickly that they had died without seeking help? Had they all died there, or had any escaped? I doubted that I would ever know.

There was nothing in this for which I could slight Seth. He had done nothing wrong and had acted wisely. Only a fool, who Seth most assuredly was not, would have investigated further. He told me later, when I finally went to absolve him of any perceived guilt in the matter and asked about their final disposition. Apparently, he had sent men to burn the cottage and its contents entirely, as even the chance of the plague being caught by some passerby who would infect others was too great to even consider salvaging the property. Guards had accompanied the men in order to prevent incautious looting, for which foresight I thanked him.

I cannot say that I shed even a single tear at the news of my family's passing. There was shock, yes, but no grieving. I found myself left alone for a few days in order to mourn, I suppose. Mistress Fairworth had one of the spit boys, an orphan called Micah, bring me my meals along with special treats while I wandered the property.

When he found me in relatively distant locations, I shared my food with him in thanks. When I did not reject his attempts at conversation, he told me of his experience losing his own parents. His mother had died birthing a brother who was stillborn, and shortly thereafter, his father had abandoned him at the gate to the manse and disappeared, never to be seen again. Mistress Fairworth had taken him in and raised him for the past five years. I remember that I liked him and that he never behaved ill toward me.

During that time, I particularly enjoyed spending time at a particular livestock pond about a half mile from the manse. Cattle and deer abounded, with the wildlife not seeming to mind our presence, either. Ducks and geese also called it home, and when I visited, I would gather some of their precious and tasty eggs to bring back to Mistress Fairworth and the delights of her kitchen. I enjoined the spit boy to keep the place a secret, to which he agreed. I would like to believe he found it as magical as I did.

Mistress Fairworth began to let me have more time to myself and would give me snacks to take along with me. She never pushed it on me, but rather would suggest that I go and take "a wee walk" and that she would take care of whatever it was I had to do. I did not ask how she managed that, I simply took advantage of the opportunity to spend some time on my own.

During these adventures, I learned about things I otherwise might not have been able to learn. For example, during one "wee walk", I discovered a distant pasture on the property that housed some of the older horses who had been turned out to graze. My innate curiosity got the best of me and I climbed over the fence and into the pasture to be closer to the big animals. One in particular, a black mare with a graying muzzle, seemed particularly fond of the apples that Mistress Fairworth would slip into my lunches. One day, I finally got up the nerve to climb onto her back after giving her a sliver of one.

Rather than reacting badly to my presence, she was downright amiable about things, and began to walk along the fence line. During our time together that day, I slipped her a few more pieces of apple, so she did not protest my presence on her back. On future visits, I remembered to bring a soft rope to slip over her nose to I had something with which to control her movements. Over time, I learned to ride bareback fairly well, and the mare and I would run across the pasture with me sticking like a tick to her broad back. I really believe that she enjoyed being useful once more instead of her boring existence grazing on a remote field.

I could not help but think about how nice it might be to own a horse of my own, but knew that I was not the kind of person who would ever to able to own much of anything. I was a servant, and servants lived at the will of their masters, owning only what the master permitted them. I rode every few days for a few months, until the master sold off the entire pastureful to a trader from a nearby town that was looking for animals the livery stable could rent out or sell.

I never had the opportunity to say goodbye to the friendly mare, but found myself hoping that her life was not too hard once she left her peaceful pasture. Thinking about it now, it was yet another time in my life where I lost someone or something I cared about and could do nothing about it.

I found it curious that I felt little to nothing emotional about the passing of my family. Perhaps it had to do with the fact that not once had any of them attempted to contact me in the time since my departure, even with the gift of a small token of their remembrance of me in either word or substance. The steward, being an honorable man, would not have lied to pretend they had in his previous visits. Therefore, for nearly three years now, my family, such as it was, had consisted of the steward, the kitchen staff and an aging wolfhound with selfish designs on the leavings of my two meals a day. I knew that I would indeed feel something were I to lose one of them, even the least of them.

It is strange how families can show up in the oddest of circumstances, and with the most curious collection of members. It is also obvious that at times, these patchwork families can be far better and have closer ties between one another than the one into which one is born. To this day, there are those who do not or simply cannot understand this concept of family.

ANNA ROSE

As a vampire, I have found myself thrown into this kind of odd family dynamic several times in my very long existence.

Chapter Three

I was sixteen or seventeen when I became more aware of the intolerance and hate between Roman Catholic Irish folk and the mostly English Anglican Catholics. Ours was a Roman Catholic household, from the lord to his family and hangers-on, as well as the vast majority of the servants. Those few servants who were not Roman Catholic were either atheists who were fortunate indeed to be allowed to serve at all instead of being hanged or even burned to death as godless evil heretics, or those who still followed the Old Religion. All had learned to live in peace within these walls, as it was necessary in order to survive from one harsh season to the next. Every so often, some fool priest or another would arrive who would attempt to exact tithes from the master. Very nearly each time this occurred, rather than deal with things himself, the master would send Seth out to meet the priest and then the steward would send him off with a few hens or if he was particularly lucky, a fat goat, but little in the way of solid coin.

We all ate well, but that was because the land was fertile and the lord's steward was shrewd when it came to managing the servants, livestock and fields. Most babes born to the servants survived to be fat and healthy children, a rarity just about anywhere in those times. A nice warm nursery was kept just off the kitchen, where a nurse and her assistant were employed to manage the infants and toddlers of the house while their mothers worked. A physician was also kept on the premises that would perform whatever barbaric form of medicine was currently being practiced as necessary, but with enough good sense that very few of his patients died as a result of his ministrations.

Frost had finally been retired when he was unable to rise from his bed for a week's time, and I was to tend to his needs in addition to my other duties. He liked to sit in the shade during the cooler part of the day, with his feet propped on a small piece of wood, which seemed to help bring down the horrific swelling to which his ankles seemed to be predisposed. Mistress Fairworth kept him stocked with tankards of not quite so weak ale and bowls of soup to which she had added extra meat to fortify him, as well as second-quality bread (retired servants commonly received third to fourth quality bread) with which he could eat the stew.

I think that I had been chosen to care for him because I was one of the few in the house who did not harbor poisonous thoughts toward the man. We did not engage in much small talk, but what few times we did spend time speaking to one another, he was able to give me some insight into his background.

Much as I could only recall having been called Siofra, Frost could only recall being called by his rather icy-sounding nickname. Perhaps he had been born with a different name, but that was something he likely would never know. When he was pressed for a patronymic, he would simply supply "White", which seemed the most appropriate, as he had never been told his true family name.

The name actually described his appearance fairly well. He had starkly white, silky-looking hair caught in a ponytail at the nape of his neck and which fell to his waist. He had impossibly white, nearly translucent skin and bluish-red almond-shaped eyes. It all gave him the appearance of one of the faerie folk, as they were often described by the itinerant storytellers who would come by and sing for their suppers, as it were. Those were amongst the times when Frost would make himself scarce, so as to not generate more talk and speculation.

The tale he had been told many years ago said that he had been born on a farm in County Cork and had almost instantly been identified as being different than normal infant children. According to what he had been told as a very small boy, his father, who felt he was a changeling by virtue of his appearance, had wanted to kill him for being some elven curse. His mother had defied his demands and had instead handed her infant child off to a wet nurse who took him to Connemara where they lived quietly in a small cottage secured with some of the money she received from Frost's mother.

The wet nurse, a woman he knew only as Nana, had cared for him until he reached the age of four or five. She had been sure that he learned how to read at least a little, by engaging the services of a skinny monk who would otherwise be sitting in front of the tavern with his begging bowl, hoping for the occasional penny. The monk had been a kind man, though a bit of a drunkard. He had finally been forced to leave town when, having spent his meager alms on a few too many pots of ale, he had no money to pay off the town's tax collector.

"I think he was called Brother Michael," he told me in his thick Connemara accent as he related this part of the tale. He grew silent for a time, lost in his thoughts, and it was several minutes before he resumed the sharing of his story.

It had been a nearly idyllic childhood, for though he had not had any friends of his own age, he wanted for nothing, his caretaker appearing to have at least some small fondness for him. He was acquainted with some few of the folk whom Nana called "friend", but they kept their distance from the child they indeed considered to have come from the dark realms.

One of her friends, a diminutive thief called Little Wat, taught Frost how to wriggle free from nearly any knot into which he might be tied and how to finesse the purse from some worthy's belt with them none the wiser to their loss. At least as long as it took for Frost to make himself scarce, anyway. Little Wat visited several times during the time he spent with Nana, so Frost was an eager and able student, picking up on many of the tips and tricks the thief provided. The best lessons Frost received from any of Nana's visitors stopped when Little Wat finally was not quick enough on his feet and was rewarded for his cunning with the keen edge of a dagger's blade.

"I remember that his voice was high and thin, and that he spoke very quickly when he was trying to talk himself out of trouble," he said. "I believe he was my first real friend."

However, all good things must end. Eventually, what little money Nana had gotten from Frost's mother for his care and shelter was exhausted. She was in poor health with no friends who might have been willing to take him on expected to visit for quite some time. After searching for a better local alternative that would have allowed her to see him, she ultimately made the decision to sell the youngster to the grasping owner of a traveling carnival, who would bill Frost to the public as one of the faerie folk. She must have reasoned that if the man paid for the child that Frost would at least be valued enough to be well fed and decently housed. Apparently, Nana had not reckoned kindness into her equation.

Frost had traveled across Ireland with the carnival as both an attraction and laborer, until he was about nine or ten years old, at which time he tired of shoveling slop and crap, and the almost daily beatings from and ravings of a lunatic master, a man known to him only as Hart. He waited until one night when his master was so far down in his cups that he passed out, gathered all the food he could carry easily and then ran as far as his short legs would carry him while the moon rode the sky.

Sadly, due to poor planning on his part, he was caught a few days later. He was then dragged back to his master, who had placed an attractive price on his healthy recovery. In order to prevent future escape attempts, Hart himself had cut off the toes of Frost's left foot upon which he now limped. He even showed me his mangled limb, which sported thick scars where the toes had once been attached. Over the years, he had learned to keep it from cracking and bleeding by rubbing it in goose grease as often as possible. He gestured at a lidded small earthenware crock that sat atop his clothes chest. It must have been where he kept the stuff. I had no desire to investigate.

It had taken a very long time for the wounds on the end of his foot to heal enough to walk on, during which time he plotted and planned his next escape attempt. Frost decided that he would no longer travel during the daylight hours, and would instead keep to the night, where he would be able to avoid easy detection. Thus, he made his plans, bided his time until his master was once more lulled into a false sense of security, and forgot to pay close attention to Frost.

It was some two years later, after his foot had healed and he had convinced his master that he was barely able to walk that he made his escape for good, this time. His master had once again gotten fall down drunk after a particularly profitable day and had left the wagon's lock off its hasp, enabling Frost's escape. This time, however, Frost also released the animals in the menagerie, as well as picking the locks of the other wagons and releasing the other human captives therein. He decided that the resulting chaos should hide his disappearance for at least a little while, anyway.

Fortunately, unlike during his previous attempt, it was very nearly a moonless night, so while it was difficult to see the ground before him, he also knew that it would make pursuit more difficult as well. He traveled until the sun began to rise, and searched until he found a small cave in which to hide, breakfasting on stale bread and part of a piece of dried meat before curling up to sleep in his cloak. He only emerged after the sun was well down. The small amount of light from the tiny sliver of moon that brightened the sky guided him through the forest. He vowed never again to be so foolish as to walk the road at any time of day.

He traveled for a good two weeks, making his way westward, gleaning food from convenient fields at night, plucking random fruit from trees and bushes, meat from quail and rabbits, and water from convenient ponds and streams. After a short time, his eyesight adjusted to nocturnal living, where his previous long time pain from the bright sunlight was a thing of the past. During the day, he hid, knowing that his wildly alien appearance would cause comment and perhaps give away his location to his former master.

Finally, he found himself at the back gate of our current master's lands, late one gray evening. After a day's long rain that had left him soaking wet and bedraggled looking, Frost had not expected anything like a warm welcome, but hoped at least for a crust that was not too badly burnt and perhaps some weak ale to wash it all down. He knocked, not really expecting a response, and so was surprised to not only get an answer, but also to meet the round dimpled face of Mistress Fairworth, peering out at him. Seeing him standing in the mud, his long hair plastered to his face, she opened the door wide and stood aside, beckoning him in. Shortly thereafter, she sat him down in her kitchen, placing a full bowl of her famously thick stew on the table in front of him, motioning for him to eat. She did not ask him any questions until he was halfway through his second bowl of stew, sopping up the juices with some of the softest and tastiest bread he had ever eaten. He very truthfully told her of his childhood, and he was startled and more than a little touched to see her eyes brimming with tears by the time he finished.

"She was the most beautiful thing I had ever seen, and I loved her instantly. I would die to protect her," he stated with calm dignity, a single tear breaking through and running, unheeded, down his cheek. "Indeed, I would have died, had she not taken me in that day."

Mistress Fairworth promised him that he would have a place within the house itself, but asked him to give her some time while she thought things through a bit more. Having nowhere else to go, he agreed, and found himself enjoying her food and hospitality during that time.

She hid him in the vast kitchen cupboard for a few weeks, until she thought of a good story to give the lord about how he had come to arrive and why adding him to the household was such a good idea. The lord, at first, had had concerns about having him on the property, but by that time, Mistress Fairworth had discovered that Frost was very good at quietly coming and going, and thus he became a spy of sorts, for when the lord had visitors who needed careful watching.

As he sat in his chair, always whittling at something, he shared with me stories of nearly being caught at his spying, and some of the important information he had discovered that he then shared with the lord. There were tales of hiding from search parties with their dogs, including the herbs and other items he had used to thwart their otherwise excellent senses of smell.

It appeared that over the ensuing thirty-five or forty years he had more than earned his place at the table and was always careful to show only the greatest respect for Mistress Fairworth. The cook had been his first and best friend in the time since he had first darkened her doorstep. She was his senior by perhaps twenty years, but that never seemed to be a problem in their friendship.

His stories made me think of all that he had accomplished whilst being different. Frost was a man who, despite his obvious differences, had very nearly made himself a ghost and legend amongst those who worked the lord's land. I found I had to respect that. Again, while I may not have particularly liked him, what closeness we had helped me to develop more of an understanding of who he was and what drove him to be the person he was now. Little did I know how much help some of his stories would be to me later in my life.

Sadly, Frost seemed to give up on life, once he was no longer of use, and it was only a short time thereafter that he passed away. Mistress Fairworth tried to keep him interested in life, and I suspect that was why she had assigned me, a young and not unattractive young woman, to get and keep his attention, but in that, she was not truly successful. Beyond the fact that Mistress Fairworth would be the only woman who held his heart, I think he felt that he had lived long enough and it was time to move onward. I believe that whatever affected his skin and eye color or lack thereof had also affected other parts of his constitution, thus, while by all rights he should have outlived Mistress Fairworth, this was not to be the case.

I had gone out to him with his evening bowl of stew, some soft bread and a tall pot of good ale. He had spent the afternoon watching the smallest children happily playing in the mud, which seemed to be something he truly enjoyed. There was a gentle smile on his face, and his hands rested on his lap, an unfinished wooden comb cradled in the lap of his leather apron. His eyes were closed, as though he had only just dozed off, but I could see that he was no longer breathing, and his lips had taken on an unfamiliar bluish cast.

Though he never said it, I think he regretted never having had children of his own, but I knew he enjoyed whittling little dollies and fashioning balls with which the boys and girls could play. Wherever he was now, I suspected he was finally, truly happy.

Mistress Fairworth saw to it that he was buried on the hill just outside the walls of the manse, where you could watch the sunset on summer nights. There were tears in her eyes as she personally took the time to wash his body and then massaged his cold twisted fingers into some semblance of straightness before wrapping him in his burial shroud. She had me help her at the last, and I used his unfinished comb to carefully tidy his hair and plait it into a neat queue, finally leaving the wooden tool in his left hand, should he need it on the other side.

"It would be ill for him should he meet his Maker with untidy hair, lass!" she said to me, as she bit off the end of the thread as she finished sewing his shroud closed for him. "I would hate to have him have to answer for that."

Another year passed, and in that time, I had fielded a few marriage proposals, all but one of which I had declined. I was not sure that they loved me, only that they felt that they needed to start a family and I was still a maiden. I know they seemed surprised when they each were politely turned down.

The single fortunate suitor, who you may recall when you hear his name, had shortly thereafter died in a fall from the roof of the manse, whilst securing tiles. Micah's screams as he fell, and the sickening *thud* as his body hit the ground will forever torment me. He was not quite dead as a result of the fall, but it only took a day or two for Death to find him and help him make his way down the path to the next plane, wherever that may be. Those one or two days were some of the longest of my life, as I begged every god I could think of for assistance, and none appeared to hear my pleas for help.

Micah had been the one human being with whom I had anything resembling a relationship and now he was gone. My heart was a dark hole and I closed down inside, allowing nothing and no one to touch me. I did my work and then went on my way, keeping to myself, a ghost that lived and breathed. The others kept away from me, which pleased me, as I had nothing at all to say to them.

I think that is when I became an atheist.

I mourned for about six months or so, daily wearing a simple black gown provided by the Cook for that purpose and most of the household left me alone, beyond what was necessary in order for me to complete my duties. During that time, Mathúin the wolfhound, elderly by canine standards, could barely walk without extreme effort on his part, thus I would give him his own full bowls of food. Mistress Fairworth, well on the road to being elderly herself, tolerated this eccentricity of mine, and was not beyond throwing a few extra pieces of good raw meat and some marrow bones in with the meat porridge in his bowl. At this point, Mathúin spent the vast majority of his time at the foot of the ladder, as advancing age had begun to prevent him from enjoying more enthusiastic adventures. He would thump his boney tail against the ground when I approached, a wide canine smile animating his graying face. His regard would often manage to thaw the cold black hole where my heart had been, and I would spend extra time scratching his great hard head and picking the parasites from his hide.

Near the end of my six months of mourning, an English lord of some sort came to visit the master. It developed that he was owed a large sum of money by our lord and had been for quite some time. He had tired of waiting on multiple promises of payment on that debt, so now he was here in the flesh, demanding a portion of my master's property instead of good gold and silver coin that might never appear. Knowing from longtime castle gossip that my lord was always short on pennies, it seemed a wise decision to me.

After being offered cattle and durable goods in payment, he had loudly declared that several years' interest on the original monies demanded even more in repayment, and thus required that some of the household staff leave with him. As a result, we servants were trotted out for inspection, with the visitor checking teeth and limbs for soundness, having us run back and forth as he watched to be certain those he chose were not cripples, then gestured one way or another as he decided which of us he wished to accompany his steward back to his own lands. I heard whispers of great arguments between the master and this English lord during this whole process, with protestations of poverty on the part of my lord.

Most of the normal leeches had left the premises, apparently feeling that by staying, they endangered their own holdings by virtue of their relationship with our lord, and this could very well have been true. In fact, they had scattered to their own homes as soon as talk of debt collection was uttered, some leaving their servants trailing along behind them in their rush to escape the English lord's net.

Perhaps a week after this Englishman came calling; I found myself on a cart bound for a new home a few days' slow journey from the far eastern side of the county, where I had lived the past several years, to the more northerly area of County Kerry around the barony of Corkaguinie. By dint of much arguing and pleading, and then finally, rather pathetic tears, I had managed to include Mathúin in the odd little caravan of servants and goods. I knew that he would not survive long without my extra care, and I must admit to feeling a debt of gratitude for his keeping me safe all these years. I surely could not abandon him now.

"What good is he to the lord now? He is only another mouth to feed. I will take full responsibility for him and you will not need to be bothered with the care and upkeep of an elderly dog," I told him, I thought reasonably. Of course, "care and upkeep" were not in the equation, as had I left Mathúin behind, he would quickly have been slain out of hand. Animals that were unable to work were a burden on the household, thus they were not permitted to live. I had given him a painless solution and rid him of another responsibility.

"Then he is yours, girl. Keep him by you and slip him into the cart when the Master is not watching. While I understand what you have told me, he might look askance at your taking the dog along." To my surprise, he actually went so far as to tousle my hair amiably before he turned away to care for the blue bitch who had whelped only the night before. She had been hidden carefully away when my new lord had swept through the place, as the Houndsman had been carefully breeding this line for some twenty years now and had no desire to lose this litter of pups to the man.

So when we left, Mathúin rode in the cart in which I kept my few belongings, and had in fact lain atop them, as if he knew of the treasures concealed within my tattered blanket and had determined to keep them safe. Taking the Houndsman's sage advice, I covered Mathúin with my other, newer blanket until we were far enough away that the old lord would not notice.

Mistress Fairworth came to see me off, care package of dried meat and bread in her hands. She patted Mathúin on his massive head, presenting him a long shinbone that still contained its marrow and that held not a small amount of meat and gave me into his able care. The dog licked her face in gratitude and proceeded to gnaw on his tasty treasure. She laughed, wiping his slobber away with the hem of her apron, then enfolded me in a hug, the aroma the lilac water she wore filling my nostrils. I turned away before she could see my own tears, but both of us were sniffling as we parted company.

"Take care of her Mathúin," she said to the dog from over her shoulder, surprising me by using my private name for him. She rushed away to hide in the relative safety of her kitchen, as she called over her shoulder: "Don't let her come to harm!"

I walked beside the cart, which was pulled by one of the young cows my new lord had acquired during his visit. She was not happy being used as a beast of burden, but one of the stableboys kept a firm hand on the rope tied to her nose-ring, so he had her undivided attention. He also took care of milking her in the morning and at night, and shared the fresh rich milk out to all of us.

About a dozen servants from the manse had been procured by our new master, ranging from stable boys to livestock handlers to kitchen servants. Some I knew reasonably well and others with whom I had only a passing familiarity that allowed me to recognize them, but I was unable to call their name immediately to mind.

A few of my fellow travelers attempted to start conversations as we went, but I did not encourage their attentions because I did not feel like engaging in small talk and mindless gossip. I guess I had become a hard woman at a very young age, and so I was not particularly fond of female companionship or gossip. The sudden upheaval had been very upsetting and I was left feeling a bit antisocial. No one dared approach the contents of the cart unless I was there to restrain and soothe my self-proclaimed guardian. At night, I slept curled up against the warmth of his old but still hard-muscled body, knowing I was completely and utterly safe in his watchful care.

Seth had somehow unearthed an old bone brooch in the shape of an oak tree, in a reasonable state of repair, which he had concealed within a travel packet of dried meat and hard bread. I was glad that I had not discovered the brooch until I was well along the road, as my sudden burst of fresh tears would have given away the sentiment that took me as I beheld this very special gift. I recall having attempted to decline the packet, but Seth had insisted that I accept it, pretending concern that I might have inadequate nourishment along the way. He had taken the place of the father I had lost, and in fact was in many ways a far better and more loving parent than I had known in the first stage of my life. I do not believe he felt a parental connection with me, but one closer to that of a doting uncle.

An otherwise unburdened man on a good horse could traverse the distance from Iveragh to Corkaguinie in less than a day's time, however the sheer size and mechanics of this undertaking meant that it would require more care and thus more time. Surprisingly, even though we were forced to keep to a relative crawl, we had no encounters with highwaymen or their ilk, thus we arrived at our new home in fairly short order.

I was more than a little awed when first I laid eyes on it. We had approached it from a hill, so my first glance at it was from that vantage. Looking down, it seemed to take up a large portion of the horizon, and I found myself wondering how many servants were needed to run it competently.

The thing was much larger than my previous home, and was in fact a castle. It was most definitely much older than the lord who now claimed it, and had probably taken the lifetime of at least one lord, if not two or three, to complete. At least two dozen mature oak trees ringed the periphery of the exterior of the castle grounds, and it was obvious that the lord had people harvesting the acorns, as I could see little to no evidence of their existence on the ground beneath them. I could see that a small orchard stood to the side of the leftmost wall, so I assumed that he grew what fruit he could on his own property. My stomach growled as I wondered what kinds of fruit grew in that orchard, as I had always enjoyed crisp apples and juicy peaches, though they had been a very rare treat, as my old master had not cultivated fruit on his property.

Within a few weeks of arriving and after cultivating the goodwill of the head housekeeper, a Saxon immigrant called Greta, I was designated a chambermaid, which was not what I had trained to be all these years, but the new lord apparently felt some caution at the thought of eating anything his new chattel might present him. His existing cook, a foul old biddy with few teeth and fewer positive qualities to recommend her, stuck to fairly simple and bland fare such as boiled beef and bread with the occasional cabbage or turnip soup when the weather was especially cold.

Unlike at our previous residence, where we had wanted for nothing, nutritionally, servants for this particular lord subsisted on stale bread and thin vegetable broth, with a small piece of some sort of unidentifiable meat at least once a week. I took advantage of any opportunity to steal into the orchard and glean forgotten apples from the ground and the trees. They were a welcome addition to my sparse diet. There were no peaches there, but apples would keep quite well for a long while, if carefully stored in a cool, dry place.

Remembering what I had been taught by Mistress Fairworth during my years in her kitchen, I made a point of gathering edible greens where I could find them and supplementing my diet with those. They did not taste as good as they would have had they been cooked, but I knew my teeth were still firm in my gums.

Cook, as she appeared to have no other name, was not beyond assigning beatings to those whom she felt had stolen from her meager larder, whether they had or not. For that reason alone, I was happy that I was now a chambermaid, and not expected to spend time within Cook's domain. That did not mean that I did not have at least one beating at her hand during my time there, but at least I had much less chance of experiencing one than, say, her cross-eyed spit boy, Pol.

SIOFRA

Mathúin slept with me on my bed, as he afforded a bit more warmth within the cold stone walls of the building. I would glean whatever leavings I could for Mathúin, who relied upon me for sustenance, and several times, I chose to go hungry, rather than allow him to starve. I could tell that he did not much care for the fare, but he was apparently smart enough to appreciate his good fortune, and would lick his bowl completely clean when given it. I had cajoled a massive shinbone from the castle's butcher, which had promptly gone to the dog. His teeth and tongue were still in good enough shape to tease the marrow out from the center of the bone. It could take him three or four days to make the entire bone disappear. In payment for this periodic largess on the part of the butcher, I would wash his clothing and took special care to return them to as pristine a condition as possible. This earned me at least a shinbone a week, as well as periodic delicacies such as liver (both beef and chicken) and sweetbreads.

The butcher offered me even more frequent "gifts" if I would warm his bed at night, but I put him off with suggestions that I had made some promise to his god regarding chastity. Fortunately, he accepted this lie and I was spared his continued importuning to be his whore.

One good thing about my new location and position was that I was given my own cell within the walls of the castle, whereas the new kitchen staff had pallets on the kitchen floor. My cell was perhaps six by ten feet, but that was enough for me to have a comfortable bed, a place for a shelf holding my things, and a locking chest at the foot of my bed for my personal items. A small inset in the wall proved the perfect place to store the apples and other random foodstuffs I collected, provided I replaced the loose bricks that concealed it from view. I had no idea why someone would have placed a hidey-hole in the small room, but I did not call it to anyone's attention, since I had no desire to have anyone check its contents. Technically, what I was doing was stealing, and I

47

could very well lose my life for taking those apples, but I knew I needed the nutrition, so I took the chance of being discovered.

My station was certainly not high enough to warrant a fireplace of my own, but I was still happy for the security of stone walls and the ability to finally have a lock to protect my possessions, with a key for myself, and a key for the steward, Gath, who was expected to maintain the lord's laws within the castle. Every fortnight or so, Gath would come to my chamber, unannounced, and go through my chest to be sure I was not taking anything, thus I was glad for the inset that housed my more important possessions.

I watched the other chambermaids very closely to learn my new position as quickly as I could manage. Having just gotten new and better lodgings, it would have been terrible to be relegated back to the kitchen and the stables. Thus, I learned to beat the rugs and bed furs clean, proper disposal of the night's soil, and other chores appropriate to my status.

I was glad that someone else took care of maintaining and banking the fires as necessary, as I had never been very gifted in that department and, honestly, had no desire to find myself powdered black with soot and ashes. Therefore, instead of me, the ash boy, a skinny and diminutive child called Flip, was generally the one covered from head to toe in soot, his arms and fingers sporting countless splinters in various stages of festering and healing. He was a decent child overall, and I would sometimes spend some of my free time picking the offending splinters of wood from his skin with the one precious bone needle I owned and washing the wounds clean with boiled water. In return, he would take Mathúin out for a slow walk in the afternoon so that the dog could relieve himself somewhere other than the stone floor of our room. I also gave him a place to hide during those times when the resident bully, Clive, a burly spit boy of about eleven, tried to establish dominance, and when he was not turning the night's joint over the fire, he would seek out victims upon whom to exact tribute.

While still a bully, Clive was very wisely afraid of the big dog that greatly appreciated Flip's daily visits, and sported a fine set of healed over tooth marks to prove it.

Clive had even tried threatening me a few times, but when I continued to laugh at his threats of violence and then in a final desperate attempt to gain my acquiescence, revenge, he finally gave up. One does not much feel like bristling and showing one's teeth when the intended recipient of those threats does not appear to take them seriously. Infant and child mortality rates in this time were terrible, with a large percentage of infants rarely surviving until the point they were able to walk, and then others who survived infancy dying before reaching puberty, so I could understand from whence some of his behavior came. Clive was an orphan who, unlike poor Frost, had stood at the gate for a week, begging for food and shelter some five years earlier until someone had finally relented and allowed him to enter the grounds, and thus had no real status beyond what he could create for himself. The other boys shunned him, as he was the sole male assigned to kitchen duties, despite the fact that his own position in the kitchen gave him access to potentially much tastier fare than they, as stable and yard boys, could hope to get without inside help.

Over time, I was able to tame tow-headed Clive somewhat, and he and Flip eventually became friends. This not only helped Flip to stay safe, but also gave Clive a bit of status gleaned from his friendly relationship with the ash boy and the massive dog who listened to no one but the odd slip of a girl whose job it was to tend the castle's frequent guests. They were about the same age, so it was appropriate that they become friendly with one another. I was glad that I could help make that happen, every small victory I could claim being precious to me. I had gone from being an unwelcome and inconveniently female individual in a genetically-related family to being a member of first one extended albeit unrelated but reasonably happy family and had then gone with some of that new family to yet another place where I was creating even more family members. It gave me a sense of power that I knew I would never have had if I were still under the thumb of my natural family.

I tended one part of the upper guest wing of the castle, which housed guests with a higher status than the average visitor. My duties included the care and maintenance of two full sets of suites and a small common room. I was required to keep them in constant readiness for visitors, and in fact, my own quarters were off the common room and next to the night kitchen, which had been installed for the convenience of any guests. I was not responsible for preparing meals, however I was required to procure and serve off hours victuals if the guest did not bring their own servant or servants to perform those kinds of functions. Fortunately, most guests brought their own help, which allowed my life to remain quiet, providing that I otherwise completed my assigned duties.

Then, there were those who had visited more than once for whom I found that I dreaded their return. These were nobles and others who came alone but were what would today be called "high maintenance". I would often find myself being run ragged in the course of trying to keep them happy. I had no choice as to whether or not I would satisfy their every whim, as the lord of the castle quite literally had the power of life and death over me. A guest could beat me to death out of hand, and as long as that guest paid whatever restitution the master required, there was no further concern.

There had been Lady Bernice and her retinue. She was a distant cousin of the lady of the castle, and demanded an entirely different board than that received by the rest of the castle's inhabitants, claiming a delicate constitution. Thus, she subsisted on lean meat broths containing vegetables boiled to the point that they fell into a very thin and watery porridge. She visited twice in two years for about a month's time for each visit. She was not too terribly bad.

There was Harold MacKenzie, Lord Prestwick's fool of an uncle. Although he was given the use of the guest rooms and its contents, he could often be found sleeping in the stable with his rock of a warhorse, Blackamoor. For some reason, the Lord of the castle felt that I had some control over how and where his uncle would spend his time, so I suffered not at the hand of MacKenzie, but the Lord, himself. At least I was able to tempt the man with sweet breakfasts and hearty suppers, carefully picking the best of the morning pastries and the best pieces of the night's joint that I was able to slip out of the kitchen. I introduced him to the joys of the simple potato as well. I would boil a few at night to go with his meat, which he would then drown in the juices from the joint and finally end up licking his plate clean. Once he discovered the potato, the man apparently no longer had any use for the trencher that was a part of meals.

At this moment in time, we were being graced with the presence of an English military man who had little use for the Irish, of which fact he had made me painfully aware more than once. He had arrived with no advance word of his pending arrival and come riding as through the devil himself had sent out the Wild Hunt to harvest his soul. His batman, a man called Bannister, took care of tea and the Colonel's uniforms, so my only real duties were to keep the suites orderly and perfectly clean.

Rather than rushes on the floors of his and the upper guest quarters, the master had caused to be installed in the common room great handwoven rugs of exotic origins. I knew they were terribly expensive, as I was reminded more than once that my value was not an atom compared to their minutely rendered beauty. Thus, I made certain that Flip exercised the greatest care when sweeping out the massive fireplace in the common room, rolling the carpet away from the fireplace's mouth and laying a wide sheet across the flagstones to catch any stray ash or splinters of wood.

A day earlier, Colonel Bigod, for that was his name, had struck a stableboy a rocking blow for not grooming his heavily lathered and exhausted mount to the Colonel's exacting standards and had left the boy concussed with serious balance issues. I could only hope the child was able to recover from the damage he had received.

It seemed that the Colonel had left behind him a trail of anger and resentment, as within a day or two of his arrival, large groups of armed Irishmen and women began to arrive on the perimeter of the castle's grounds. These were not just simple peasants with only pitchforks and scythes, either. There were a few firearms such as flintlock pistols, bows, arrows and swords in amongst the fast growing mob. One of the washerwomen told me that she had seen several ragged uniforms within the ranks of the mob, so I assumed that Colonel Bigod had indeed burned some bridge or perhaps several bridges behind him. Now some very rightly angry persons had come along to exact their revenge upon him and damn whoever was caught in the crossfire.

I was fortunate that I was enclosed within the castle proper, as those caught outside were either conscripted into the service of the mob, or they met with deaths either simple or grisly, depending upon the situation. However, it was only a matter of time before they would have us, as we only had so much in the way of stores to sustain ourselves during a siege.

One day, a few weeks into the siege, I heard through the grapevine that a group was apparently building catapults and other siege engines outside the walls, those oaks that were not already earmarked as future firewood were slowly being harvested for the materials needed. I wondered how long it would be before they began employing the engines against the innocents inside who had taken no part in whatever evil Colonel Bigod had committed, but would be forced to suffer for his sins.

Over a period of perhaps two months and at least a week's worth of bombardment by the siege engines, things became increasingly dire within the castle. Rations became tighter and I found myself limited to a diet of cabbage water, weak ale and coarse black bread once a day. Some of the servants climbed the walls and ran off in the night until the lord, furious over the defections, ordered that the stores with which those walls had been lined be pulled away and brought indoors, thereby removing one avenue of escape. In their place, pots of pitch had been set along the tops of the walls in the areas most vulnerable to invasion, in anticipation that at some point, the rebels would attempt to gain access through those avenues. Dried dung and other combustibles from the midden heap were placed beneath the pitch pots to be used if and when things became dire enough to warrant the melting of the contents and subsequent pouring of the resulting molten liquid upon the attackers coming up the walls from below. I could not help but wonder how, once such an invasion began, that they would have the time to light the fires and heat the pitch enough for it to melt well enough to pour, but siegecraft was not my forte, so I said nothing.

I also learned that the fool of a Colonel had caused five villages to be burned to the ground because the inhabitants refused to accept English rule. While many had survived the fires, many others had been seriously injured or lost in the conflagrations, and their families and friends had responded with understandably terrible rage. Even several of the Colonel's former men, especially those who had their own families and children, horrified by what had occurred, had defected and allied themselves with the survivors. Thus, there was some military experience behind the siege which kept things from falling apart on the rebels' side of things. The lord of the castle was himself horrified by what had been done in the name of King and Country, however, being a Loyalist, he would never himself become a rebel, thus surrendering Colonel Bigod to those without was never in question. Perhaps, if it had been, my own fate would not have been what it became.

Chapter Four

I went to sleep that night practically wrapped around Mathúin, who was suffering far more from the effects of poor nutrition than I. His ribs were plain to see, as his body had consumed what little fat it had left, so he trembled with the cold as he slept. I made certain that the blanket covered not only me but his body as well. He had been my friend for a great many years now, and I knew his remaining time with me was not going to be much longer; however, it was not in me to make his final days any more miserable than they needed to be, so I offered as much comfort as I could while I was still able.

The siege was nearing an end. The lord of the castle had taken an arrow to his gut whilst manning the wall late one afternoon some weeks earlier, and even though the castle's physician had seen to and treated the wound as quickly as possible, it was fairly evident that some of the lord's internal organs had been damaged by the projectile. The stench of infection had appeared quickly and the lord had devolved into mad ravings and screams of agony, sleeping but little. The physician did what he could to try to rid the lord's body of the infection using leeches and bleeding to remove the infection from his body, to no avail. At this point, even my dear elderly Mathúin would quite easily outlive the stinking lunatic who moaned, writhed and withered in the front hall of the castle, wrapped in the once fine furs that were now crusted and stinking with the weeping effluvia of his fatal infection.

I found that I was doing a lot of sleeping lately, now I believe it had something to do with my body's attempts to keep as much energy in reserve as possible. One of the kitchen helpers who remained was bringing me what food she could. Flip had run off with his boon companion, not that I could say that I blamed either of them for looking to their own safety. In fact, it had been their defections that had finally made the Colonel a bit mad. The male servants had been fitted with manacles, which limited their movements in an effort to keep them from taking advantage of breaches in the fortifications to affect their own escapes. In addition, the yard's wolfhounds had been kept on the hungry side, so they were not beyond attacking even the castle's own denizens in an effort to secure some kind of nourishment.

Anyhow, that night, I was so debilitated that I felt rather than heard the great crash which brought down the south wall of the castle's yard. Rather than seeking a safer place to hide, I found myself stumbling down the hall toward the source of the commotion. People whose faces I did not recognize were pouring in through the breach and making their way into the castle. They seemed to ignore my weak stumbling down the corridor, and I leaned hard against the wall when I was jostled especially hard by a passing soldier who held a great bloodied sword in one hand. My legs were unable to hold me upright, and I fell hard to my hands and knees.

Undaunted, I began to crawl toward the main hall where the lord reclined upon his deathbed. Some sense of duty impelled me forward, though even now I could not tell you why. I had no loyalty for the crazy old man, so perhaps it had to do with knowing that in his current condition, he was helpless to defend himself. All I can tell you is that it took what seemed forever before I arrived, my palms and knees scraped and bloodied from their rough journey across the flagstones. When I looked, I saw a dark cloaked and hooded figure standing above him, and my mind screamed at me that something was very wrong about this tableau, encouraging me to run away as quickly as I possibly could.

It was too bad that I was terrible about taking advice, even my own.

Using what little strength I had left, I launched myself from the floor toward this mysterious figure, shouting at him to move away, to leave the lord to his death. Imagine my surprise when the man reached out a single hand to practically snatch me out of the air and then to clutch me against his chest. I felt a low chuckle rumble in his chest and then the stranger and I were away in some dark corner of the room, away from the hullabaloo. I was too exhausted after using that small burst of energy to fight free, so I hung there in his arms, waiting for whatever fate awaited me.

"You have still some fight left in you, eh, girl? You must have strong blood indeed!" he grated out with an odd accent before I felt a bone grinding pain in my shoulder and then the sensation of warmth pouring down the front of my gown. Cold lips pressed against the wound and I felt myself being sucked up through the hole in my flesh and down into the body of the creature which held me tight. My very soul cried out in anguish at what was happening to me, and begged me, nay, pleaded with me, to do everything I possibly could to save it from death. It just was not ready to enter the Afterlife.

Somewhere, I found the determination not to go quietly into the Abyss, and thus I began to scratch and kick at the one who held me. He put up his free hand to stop my attempts to defend myself, and I grabbed it, then brought it to my mouth and bit down, hard, breaking the skin and causing the bitter fluid he might laughingly call his blood to ooze into my own mouth. Perhaps hoping that it might cause him to let go, I continued to chew at his flesh, mindless of the vile substance that coated my tongue and trickled down my throat. I was wrong, of course, and despite my best efforts to deter him, instead fell unconscious as he finished swallowing the last of what I had to give. The last thing I heard was titanic growling, felt some sort of heavy impact that resulted in my falling to the floor and the creature's startled oath as blackness took me.

Chapter Five

Dreams.

Dreams of screams and wailing and horror. Pleas for mercy. A terrible ear-piercing scream. The sounds of pitched battle and finally silence. A deep, all-encompassing silence, which I found mercifully welcome and peaceful. I could finally rest, yes?

At some point, I roused slightly, although I was unable to open my eyes. I could tell that my bowels had let loose and that I was lying in my own filth, as happens when something dies, so I surely must be dead! Why was the afterlife taking so very long to take me into its embrace? Would I forever be trapped in this half-alive state, aware of my surroundings, but unable to act? I silently cried out to all gods that might be listening to free me from this awful inertia. Were they listening? Did they care about a mere servant girl? Once more, I drifted away into the blessed darkness, praying for an answer.

I woke to the feeling of a warm tongue lapping at my face and shoulder, and my eyes opened to behold Mathúin making a determined effort to clean the area around the wound that should have resulted in my death. Had that been his growling that I had heard? Surely not, as this did not seem to be the Mathúin I had known for so many years! This Mathúin seemed filled out and had none of the signs of advanced age that I had come to know in my four-legged friend, this one was perhaps no more than a year or two in age. Surely this was another animal of similar breeding.

He stopped his licking and sat on his haunches, watching me with his familiar eyes and I knew that somehow, this was the same dog. I reached out a hand and he leaned forward to sniff at it and give it a cursory lick before sitting back once more.

The multiplied stench of sewage, death and decomposition assailed me, and somehow I knew that Mathúin and I were the only living things who remained within the castle that were larger than a cat. It was a sad realization which only made me feel even more bereft, if that were possible. Alone again, the few friends I had managed to gain over so many years gone as the result of starvation and violence. Why did I even bother to try to create those connections when so far, life had shown me that all such attempts were ultimately useless?

"What happened? Why am I still alive?" I asked the dog, even though I knew there was no way he could reply. It is probably a normal thing for someone to do. Maybe I just wanted to hear the sound of my own voice in the unnaturally silent hall. "I should have died. Why didn't I?"

Blearily, I looked about me and saw bodies in various states of both wholeness and decay. It was clear where Mathúin had taken some of his meals, not that I could really blame him. Perhaps it was only our closeness, sealed so many years ago, that had kept him from adding me to the list of sources from whom he could gain nourishment. Thinking about what he had been eating, I pushed him away to stop his licking.

With a strength that surprised me, I rose to my feet and looked down at Mathúin, who returned my regard with an open-mouthed toothy smile and a slow wag of his tail. His teeth shone sharp and white in his mouth, though his lower left fang was still broken from when he had been kicked by one of the guardsmen. So his rejuvenation was not perfect but still very jarring.

He truly seemed happy to see me, which gave me a feeling I had not experienced in a very long time, but still I was confused. Was I alive? Was I dead? Was this some hellish half-life to which I had been sentenced for some portion of eternity?

It was apparent from the chaos around me that all within these walls had been done to death, so I could not understand why I had been allowed to live. All of the staff, males and females alike, were dead, and even the old lord had not been allowed to die in his own bed of the mortal wound which had already been drawing away his life like some fetid succubus feasting on his soul. One unfortunate glance showed that someone had taken the time to remove the lord's head from his shoulders, and then had placed the head down by his knees, facedown. I turned away, sickened by the sight.

There were maggots, flies and beetles everywhere, scouring the rotting flesh from the bodies that lay all around me. The familiar faces of so many people who would speak and laugh no more were bloated and grotesque to behold.

The first thing I wanted to do was to scrub the filth from my body. I stripped out of my ragged, feces and urine-stained gown, grabbed a relatively clean rag from the floor and made my way to the trough in the kitchen yard, clambering into the water without a second thought and began scrubbing madly at my skin. It hurt to be so very rough on myself but I could not stand the thought of death clinging to my flesh any longer than it must.

A good half hour or so after my frantic bath began, I crawled out of the trough and stood in the sunlight, fascinated at the detail of the drops of water on my pale skin. It was as if I could see deep into the tear-shaped drops that beaded there, magnifying the pores of my skin. I do not believe I had ever noticed that before, but then, I would perhaps have had four full baths in my lifetime to that point, as I recall.

Suddenly, I felt hungry, a hunger that seemed to echo in my very bones. If I was hungry, I must still be alive! It was only reasonable. My hunger gnawed at me again and I went back inside and to the kitchen to see if I could find anything there. I grabbed an apron from one of the hooks on the wall and pulled it over my head, giving myself some semblance of decency. It was clear that the invaders had emptied the chamber and its anterooms of everything they could possibly find, so I went to my former chambers to look there. No, they hadn't found my carefully concealed store of stolen victuals!

However, when I attempted to eat some of it, I found I could not even choke it down. It was as though my throat closed up on me when I tried to swallow, and the food tasted rancid and downright vile to my tongue. Spitting it out, I searched for something to wash the taste out of my mouth and finally picked up nearly full Mathúin's water bowl, gulping down the contents. Mathúin looked at me a bit oddly and obligingly ate what I had spat onto the floor.

Dogs really have no sense of decorum.

Within a few moments of downing the water, I found myself literally drenched in sweat. The apron very quickly looked as though I had been wearing it as I bathed. I did not have the other symptoms of fever, so I was nonplussed at this turn of events. I tore off the apron and replaced it with one of the enormous cloths the cook used when making bread, wrapping it around myself like a sheath of some sort. The creative clothing did not last, however, as it, too became soaked, and I stripped it off to once again stand naked, to the smiling amusement of an eight stone wolfhound as he cocked his head at me with a look that spoke volumes.

Exhaustion overtook me and I lay down on a pile of clothing and curtains that lay in a shadowed corner. I tried to cover myself with part of one of the curtains, but found my damp skin was entirely too sensitive to tolerate its touch, so instead I lay atop the mound and drifted away into a dreamless sleep, Mathúin lying in the doorway like some stone gargoyle, watching for any potential invaders.

I do not know how long I slept, but at some point, my eyes opened and I sat up, noting that the sun was out once more, and that I could hear birds outside, both songbirds and carrion birds. Mathúin, seeing that I was awake came to me and I spent a few minutes scratching his massive head, and then went looking for something to wear. It was not as though anyone in the castle would need it. Knowing this, I actually went into the mistress' rooms and into her vast closet full of gowns, looking for something appropriate for a lady, and then realized that wandering the countryside in a gown was probably not the wisest course to take. It was perhaps safer to be taken for a lad, in fact.

Thus, I reluctantly left the mistress' chambers and went instead to the lord's, where I found a pair of black breeches in reasonable, although not perfect condition, which when belted did not fit me too badly and an off-white blouse that could be tied at the waist with a length of cord I found lying around. Shoes were a more difficult thing to locate, but I finally discovered a pair of soft leather boots that had apparently belonged to one of the household lads which did not chafe my feet too badly when I walked about in them, my feet cushioned with woolen stockings. I finished the ensemble by braiding my hair close to my head and then topping the entire display with dark brown flat cap. Mathúin sniffed at the results and wagged his approval of my appearance. When the dog has shown he approves, what more can be said? Then, the happy canine smile abruptly turned into a snarl, and Mathúin whirled away, heading down the corridor at a speed I had never before seen, but I soon caught up with him, drawn by something I could not quite define, but which drew me like the proverbial moth to a candle flame.

I was brought up short when I discovered a man in a soldier's uniform working his way through a pile of bodies on the floor, apparently looking for something to loot from what had been looted days earlier. I had actually scented him as I flew down the corridor behind Mathúin, and then hid behind a pillar and watched him, closing one hand over Mathúin's mouth to keep him silent, though the dog already seemed to know that was exactly what I wanted. I inhaled deeply, smelling the musk of the man's skin and dirty clothing. It was very nearly an intoxicating perfume to me. Not even realizing that it should be impossible for me to do so, I could hear a soft rhythmic thumping and somehow, I knew it was the sound of his heart. I felt offended that the would-be thief seemed calm in his excavations, his heart betraying his near-boredom with the proceedings.

Without thinking anything through, I stepped out from behind the pillar to make myself known. The man caught my movement and looked up, his heartbeat jumping in response to his startlement, and I watched him tense up, his hand closing around the hilt of the dirk at his waist. Oddly, this did not frighten me.

"Hello," I breathed at him, allowing a lazy smile to cross my lips, and I pulled the cap from my head. Still smiling, I loosened my hair from its braids and then shook my head slightly, allowing the wavy mass to fall loosely around my face, shoulders and back.

Entranced, the man pulled his hand away from his knife. He unconsciously extended his hand to me, looking as though he were inviting me to dance. I could hear the timbre of his heart change from the fight or flight reflex to the steady thump of arousal. A new scent was added to what had been there before, one I would eventually come to know as being that of male human pheromones.

A transparent smile that did not reach his eyes crossed his own face, and he made some noises I can only assume were meant to be reassuring. I could see that he was already beginning to pitch his tent. Perhaps he thought me to be one of the lord's daughters, attempting to escape a similar fate as the rotting dead who surrounded us.

I had never cut my hair in my life, and it was down past my buttocks, a real attention getter. I became all coquettish and slid up to him with a grace I did not remember ever having had before. As he stood, transfixed, I reached out a hand and ran my index finger down the side of this throat. I could feel his body's warmth and could feel the throb of his pulse under my fingertip. I cupped my hand slightly and stroked the curve of his jaw, watching him swallow, and seeing the bulge in his pants swell with my touch. I could feel the depth of his yearning to rape me, to force me down and shove himself repeatedly within me until he spent himself planting his diseased seed in my womb. He might even let me live, afterward, but I suspected that my continued survival was not really set in his plans. I believe he saw me as a one-night stand, as one might call it.

Some instinct I could not identify let him run his hands over my body, and I saw his expression become confused when I apparently did not feel the way he expected me to feel. He suddenly stiffened and grabbed one of my hands. I let him continue to touch my hand as he roughly rubbed it and turned it over to look at the veins of my wrist. His jaw dropped in what must have been shock, but at that time, I did not know why he had that reaction to me.

It did not matter in the least. My hunger throbbed through me like vibration of a bass drum, and I could not ignore it any longer. He began to pull away from me, but I grabbed him with the hand held and pulled him in close to me. I caught and held his eyes with my own, and he stopped trying to step back. That was when I made my move, though I still cannot tell you how I knew what I had to do.

I leaned forward as though I were going to kiss him on the lips, my hand slipping around the back of his thick neck, taking a firm grip of the hair at the nape while my other hand made as if to cup his balls through the fabric of his trousers. A moan escaped my lips as my anticipation began to overwhelm me. I am sure it could easily have been mistaken for the sound of sexual desire. Then, at the last moment, when I felt him relax into my caress and drop his guard, I instead went for his throat. I felt my upper and lower eyeteeth surging out from my gums and used them to tear a hole in the side of the man's throat. Some instinct made me immediately lock my lips around the hole, making a crude yet effective way to keep the blood from spilling away and down to the ground.

The blood poured forth from the ragged hole in a hot, thick red fountain, which I managed to avoid spilling by sucking it down like a starving babe at its mother's breast. Waves and waves of pleasure spilled over me as I drank, his blood tingling like the finest and most exotic spices as it passed over my eager tongue.

He tried to fight me off, but using a strength that surprised me, I stayed in place, even as I felt his dirk plunge into my left kidney. Instead, I yanked it out and threw it across the room, where it lodged in a wooden bust of some sort. I did not care; I was too fixated on the amazing sensations that feeding on his hot, rich living blood gave me. I truly did not want the wondrous experience to end.

I did not know it at the time, but I was refilling tissues that had lost much of their moisture at the time of and after my death. I had lain amongst the rotting corpses of the household for three days as my body changed from something living and human into what it was today: a capable and deadly machine designed for the quick and efficient acquisition of the fuel it required, which in this case, was human blood. Mathúin had spent those three days guarding my body and keeping me safe from the rodents that had always plagued the grounds. I saw the remains of his devotion, the heads and tails of curious and hungry rats, strewn about the room. However, I would not discover the three-day transition period for a long time to come.

The fingers of my left hand, which appeared to have developed talons about the same time as my fangs emerged, dug into the muscle of his neck and held him upright. He screamed in agony and I chuckled over my mouthful of flesh. I closed my eyes and reveled in the feeling of my own power as I took his life from him, drinking him down as though my own depended upon it. I was the mistress of my own existence now, and was beholden to none. I smelled the rank stink of his seed when his orgasm let loose to stain his pants. There was no echo of conscience from my mind as I killed the man who would have killed me as easily as one swats an irritating gnat, were I still human. His blood was both salty and sweet, with a flavor like the one ambrosia must have. I could feel Mathúin as he approached and the jerk as the massive animal ripped off part of the man's hand, swallowing the nearly bloodless flesh down in a single gulp.

I could not say when he stopped struggling, immersed as I was in the act of feeding and of feeling the touch of a life cradled in my arms. I could only tell you that just before he died, the flavor of his blood changed, so I stopped feeding. As his heart ceased beating, all the muscles in his body relaxed, causing his bowels let loose and foul his clothing. I dropped him to the ground and stepped away to avoid being touched by the disgusting human effluent.

As I came to myself once again, it finally dawned on me that I was no longer human. I probed at my fangs with my tongue. There were four of them, on the sharp side of dull, with the top pair being larger than the lower, but they fit together nicely when I closed my mouth, but did not distort it obviously. They were, as had been very well demonstrated, quite capable of tearing flesh. Upon inspection, I saw that my finger and toenails had both grown thicker and a bit longer, apparently designed to catch and hold prey. I was no longer the meek girl who labored for a wealthy lord. I was a predator at or near the top of the food chain. Something to be taken very seriously and most certainly not dismissed out of hand, as one might a mere servant.

Something had happened to me when that creature had fed upon me. Would this corpse that lay at my feet rise from the dead at some point as well? Without a second thought and in a single fluid motion, I tore his head from his bloodlessly pale body and threw it across the room, where it smashed into the stone wall, and the sound of his fracturing skull made me laugh a delightedly girlish laugh. Some inner voice told me that this would be an effective method of keeping him completely dead. Yes, it is okay to laugh. I know that I did.

I felt my side and discovered that the knife wound was gone, healed over completely as though it had never happened. There was not even much blood at all around the wound, which surprised me, so little, in fact, that with a small bit of mending, I could still wear it when I left. It was not until much later that I discovered that the blood I drank took some time to fully transport itself through all my tissues.

Within a few minutes, my fangs and talons had receded and looked like nothing more than regular teeth and fingernails once more. I looked at my wrists to see what had caught his attention and noticed that the veins there had shriveled almost to the point of invisibility; however, it was quite obvious that they were empty, as they did not stand out as once they had. I remembered that once upon a time, they had stood out green and blue against my flesh, creating tangible lines across the surface of my skin. Now my skin was easily twice as pale as it had been, and my veins were barely noticeable to the naked eye. The same was true of the back of my hand, creating the appearance of being very much like a finely defined china doll from France.

The lord's piggish daughter Margaret had had some china dolls of her own until her father married her off to some financially convenient lord in England, at which point they had been sold to an itinerant tinker for him to dispose of as he pleased. She had lavished much attention on the things, playing at tea parties and arranging grand balls for them at times. I was usually the fortunate one who got to clean up after she was done playing, blotting spilled tea from the floor and generally putting the solar back to its normal sense of order and tranquility.

Margaret's new husband had evinced no interest in transporting the dainty gewgaws to his manor, declaring them lovely to look at, but more than a little useless. The girl was to provide him with strong sons, not useless daughters to waste their time in frivolities and his money in getting them married off to suitable husbands. Margaret, still only fifteen or sixteen at the time of her marriage, had wept when she was taken from her family with little or nothing of her own. Thomas, her husband, had said he would provide all he felt she should require once they returned to England. There was a small part of me that had felt sorry for her as I remembered my own loss of the family I knew, but this was tempered by the knowledge that she had no idea what it was like when you are torn from your family to serve another at their pleasure.

I never saw her again. Word reached the lord a year or so later that Margaret had died in childbed, birthing a stillborn daughter. Lady Vivian, her lady mother, cried and wept for a week. Lord Philip, apparently not wanting to witness extended feminine histrionics, went hunting with one of his three sons, disappearing for a month and then coming back with a brace of doves, three quarters of a boar and a decided limp. It seemed his prize had used its tusks to good use and had torn into his thigh before finally dying. Ever after, Lord Philip remembered that boar hunt every time the weather got cold.

Shortly after her husband and son returned, Lady Vivian, bereft at the loss of her only daughter and ignored by her husband, had gone to live with her sister in London. A part of me always wondered if he ever noticed her absence. Another part of me would promptly suggest that very likely, he never noticed she was gone.

One of the sons had died of a fever a month before the arrogant Colonel Bigod arrived on the scene, while their remaining two sons had been killed while trying to escape their father's land during the early days of the siege. Or perhaps it was from the three sessions of bleeding the well-intentioned but medically challenged physician had prescribed as part of his treatment. Who knew?

Examining myself further, I saw that my hair had taken on a glossy sheen and bounce it had never had in life. I could not help running my fingers through my hair and exploring the texture of the strands. It was as though I could feel the curve and shape of each hair as my fingers pulled through them. Amazingly, it even boasted a red more vivid than it ever had been while I still breathed. It no longer had that faded look that all red hair gets from exposure to the sun, as though the light of the sun had never touched my head.

Yes, you heard that right. I had no need to breathe, and unless I put a small part of my concentration in charge of that particular act, I would stop, with no ill effects as a result. Talking required air to work properly, but unless I planned to speak or catch the scent of my surroundings, I would discover that I need not bother doing so.

Going to Lady Vivian's rooms and stripping down until I was completely nude once again, I used the polished metal mirror she had used to check herself to see how my appearance had changed. Even though it was not a perfect surface of reflection, I still got enough detail from it to know that I did not look much as I remembered I had before my apparent death and transformation.

My skin was uniformly pale, as though sun had never touched an inch of it. Looking down, I could see that old scars remained, such as the nasty one on my left shin from when I had fallen down the stairs outside Mistress Fairworth's kitchen. My hair appeared to be glossier and much fuller, my cheekbones perhaps a bit sharper, and my arms and legs almost impossibly slender. I believe the last had to do with the starvation I had endured in the last few months of my human life. My bosom was very nearly nonexistent, a result of poor nutrition and my body's consumption of its own substance as I slowly starved. Putting the mirror as close to my face as I could and still be able to focus, I could see that my eyes appeared to be the same pale green they had always been.

That night, I slept in the mistress' bed, as she obviously no longer needed it. I had never before experienced a feather bed and was quite taken by how incredibly soft and comfortable it was, compared to the blanket covered layer of rushes from which my own previous bed was composed. I rolled about in it for a time, delighted as a child might be at playing with a marvelous new toy, but exhaustion eventually took me and finally I surrendered to Morpheus' bidding.

My sleep was dreamless, the emptiness of my mind being much like blowing out a candle and being plunged into a dark, lightless room. My mind seemed to turn completely off. It made me glad that I had Mathúin to watch over me as I slept the sleep of the dead. Who knew what might have happened if someone had come upon me insensate and thought me deceased and my body in sore need of disposition? Would I waken when it was already too late and discover myself deposited firmly underground with only worms and grubs to keep me company, or worse perhaps, awakening to find myself aflame upon a funeral pyre? It was truly a terrifying thing for me to consider, and I decided then and there that in the future, I must always act with care when choosing my resting place.

Its funny how becoming a vampire, though I did not know that was what I was at that time, can completely change how you look at the world. No, I was not some ravening fiend plotting my next feeding, but even as a fledgling, I knew I had to be careful. I was learning about any limitations my new aspect might place upon me in a manner much like on the job training and preferred to have as much control over things as I could arrange.

I knew also that I could not remain where I was because there was not another living human being anywhere in the vicinity upon whom I would in any way feel comfortable feeding upon. Much like the early nomadic human hunter-gatherers in the days before agriculture was discovered, one goes where the food is if one wants to survive, rather than remaining where it is not. Also, there were greater chances that if I remained here, I would end up dining on someone I knew and might even care about a wee bit. That was not anything I desired to do any time soon if I had was given any choice in the matter.

In further thinking about it, it made sense to me that moving somewhere that had civil unrest or outright war would be my best destination. I would have to do some research to find where that particular destination might be. For now, moving to the city would be an excellent idea, with Dublin, as I had heard it described by those who had been there as teeming with all manner of humanity, a useful and sensible destination under my particular circumstances.

And so I reluctantly bid goodbye to my former home and the wondrous feather bed housed within it. I needed to travel to a more appropriate and inhabited part of the world if I was to survive very long. The manse was left to the vermin who feasted on the bodies within and without, and the elements themselves feasted upon the manse itself until in but a few decades, all that remained was a shattered stone ruin.

Chapter Six

My travels were interesting, to say the least. I moved on my own two feet and liked it that way. Going slowly allowed me to experience the world in an entirely new way. In a very short time, I learned to listen to the sounds of the animals and insects around me, as they were an effective early warning system in the event something serious was ahead. Mathúin spent a lot of time running freely, which had to be wonderful, considering that he had only recently been reborn after being weak and starving for so very long. Because of our blood connection, we could now feel one another's minds, so if I needed him, he was back in a flash.

It was not as though I could read his mind. It was more a sharing of sensations and moods. I knew when he was content or angry and if he was hungry or sated, and I'm sure he knew the same from my own mind. I could feel his fondness for me and an unspoken acceptance of me as his mistress, but in a way much stronger than a Houndsman for his pack. Mathúin would quite literally do anything necessary to keep me safe, even if it lead to his own very permanent death. It was a very frightening and humbling thing for me to consider, really.

A few times during the first few days, I met travelers on the road and spent a little time with them to break the monotony. I met with two single travelers, but only one of the two proved to be untrustworthy. He became my next meal. Of course, I waited until he tried raping me before I acted. Perhaps if he had left me alone, I might have allowed him to live. Oh, well.

My reaction to his attack was automatic, with little thought to what I was doing. I believe it was a combination of protecting myself and needing to feed, so it was not a pretty or particularly graceful thing to behold. The man had waited until Mathúin was off hunting for his dinner to attack me, apparently believing my slight size reflected a lack of strength. There was no finesse to my response, only instinct.

"You're not fooling anyone, girlie," he laughed as he stepped up behind me and looped an arm around my neck, pulling back in an attempt to cut off my air and make me faint. "I want a piece of what you have to offer!"

I suspect he had tried this particular tactic in the past, but this time, he was outmatched. Obviously overconfident and thus woefully careless, he had not noticed that I was not breathing in the first place. Taking advantage of his terminal foolishness, I gagged a bit and then pretended to swoon, which made him relax his hold. He shoved me to the ground and began to try to pull my pants down around my ankles. At that point, I twisted in his grasp, hissing like an angry snake and bit at his face, sinking my fangs wherever they might gain a purchase.

The result was that my mouth closed on the area around his nose and when I pulled backward, I took a large portion of his face with me. Spitting the raw flesh out onto the ground, I watched the blood rush to what was left of his face and pour down his front. His nose and some of its cartilage had come away with his upper lip, leaving his upper gums and teeth exposed like some horribly bloody skull.

The man screamed a high keening sound like that of a wounded rabbit and tried to push me away in a bid to escape me, but he was unsuccessful. I wrapped my hands around his throat and pulled him close, shifting him sideways just a tiny bit to make things easier for me. I bit an opening in his carotid artery and began to drink deeply.

The keening continued until he finally passed out from blood loss, which made it easier for me to continue feeding. It seemed that anger could spark my hunger, and at this point, my body craved his blood. When his blood's flavor changed, as it had with my first feeding, I dropped him to the ground and left him there for those in the area who would appreciate the fresh meat.

SIOFRA

Mathúin had arrived shortly after I began feeding, and once he saw that I had been able to defend myself, kept his distance and amused himself elsewhere. There was a half-eaten rabbit dangling from his jaws and he took the opportunity to finish his prize. When he saw that I was done with my own meal, he trotted over and urinated on the cooling body, his opinion on the matter quite clear.

I found the closest source of water I could and bathed myself and rinsed my blouse as best as I was able before continuing on my journey. My years of experience taking care of others' clothing came into good use in removing the blood from my blouse, so I was fortunate in that regard. A few hours spent hanging off some tree branches in the sun dried my blouse at which time I put it back on and we were ready to resume our journey, none the worse for wear.

I let down my hair, combed it out until all the knots and tangles were gone, and then re-braided it tightly, tucking it up under my cap to conceal its length. I really would have to see about cutting it soon, so that I did not have to keep it braided all the time as I was loath to do so. I enjoyed my hair, especially with its new volume and shine, and the idea of cutting it to shoulder length was an almost painful thing to consider, but sometimes, we do not have a choice in what we must do to survive.

I kept to the farce that I was a youth traveling on foot to Dublin, and most seemed to accept that at face value, though some few needed to be dissuaded from forcing themselves upon me. Those had an excellent chance of becoming afternoon tea. Sometimes, however, Mathúin would approach, fangs bared, unfriendliness plain upon his furry face, and that unwanted suitor would usually think better of his original intention and beat a hasty retreat to destinations hitherto unplanned.

I even traveled for a day with a troupe of players who, once they discovered I was female, entreated me to join with them on a more permanent basis.

"You are already doing an excellent job of pretending to be a man! Why, you could stay with us and we could all travel and work together!" exhorted Tim the Mime. He rubbed his hands together in avaricious expectation of riches to come, I suppose. "How will you keep safe traveling as a lone girl?"

It was funny how he had already forgotten my successful travel in this guise thus far. That is something I must say about how much I appreciate modern times in the western world and the overall lack of paternalistic thinking where lone female travel is concerned. You pat them on the back, tell them to periodically update whatever online social networking forum they might use, and send them on their way. Such was not the case in 1600's Ireland.

"I do appreciate your kind offer, all of you, but I have people I must meet and they are expecting to see me within the next fortnight. I cannot leave them waiting and wondering after me. I am sure you can understand that. I would hate to see them accuse you of having kidnapped me." I replied oh so reasonably. No, vampires do not possess the power of suggestion, unless they are already hypnotists of course—but even then, you still cannot make someone do something they would not normally do. We vampires simply must learn to be quick thinkers and to sound reasonable when we press our case. "Maybe you could let me know what it was that made you know I'm a woman…"

Sorry to burst your bubble, dear reader, if you were expecting me to just give them The Hairy Eyeball and just make them do whatever it was I wanted them to, all those old silver screen era vampire antics to the contrary. This is reality, not convenient and easy to resolve fantasy.

I was lucky that time, and my words appeared to do the trick. Actors were not held in very high regard, being thought to be very nearly as untrustworthy as the thieving vagabonds who periodically came through villages across the whole of Ireland in their gaily decorated and noisily belled wagons, so encounters with the local constabulary were to be avoided at all costs.

After a few short lessons on maintaining a more masculine appearance and a shared meal of meat and rough dark bread, with mine surreptitiously going to Mathúin since I was unable to eat it, I bid them farewell and went on my way, but by a slightly different route at first, in order to avoid any well-intentioned but ill-advised pursuit. I actually did not particularly like racing on foot at breakneck speed as I was now able, even though Mathúin kept up easily. I liked to take my time, if I could, but this was a circumstance where I needed to cover several miles worth of road ahead of my acquaintances, so this time, I was forced to do so. Once I was about a day's travel in front of them, I rejoined the road and continued at my sedate and unhurried walk.

A few more such encounters and it was not long before I decided that I truly preferred to travel alone. I hated having to explain myself and to be so very careful to conceal my feminine nature. This was a time when women were considered chattel, or property. Your father essentially sold you to your new husband as part of what was a financial arrangement. Yes, Irish women officially had more rights than, say, an English woman or a Scottish lass, but when it came down to it, girls and women tended to bend to the will and wishes of their fathers

Although I had many opportunities to feed during my travels, I held out as long as I could before I finally fed once more, and then it was on some poxed and lonely farmer who lived alone on his smallholding. He apparently thought, once he divined that I was female, that I would abandon all hope of a better existence and spend the rest of my time with him. Of course, he would be terribly disappointed. After our little dance of death, I left him, as with my first feeding, separated from his head by a wide margin. In fact, I believe I left it on the far side of his cornfield, while his body rested very near his front door. Mathúin satisfied himself with a lick and a bite from the raw ruin of the man's neck once I removed his moon-eyed head. It appeared to be some part of our strange bond that he could take his pound of flesh, as it were, from my kills. As I had no use for the flesh, he would have no argument from me on the subject.

I most often slept in the ruins of old castles, abandoned farmhouses and the like. Mathúin would stand guard as I rested. Although I found I could travel during the day as easily as in the night, I found it much easier to pass as male when fine details of my features were much more difficult to see. In addition, I felt a certain oneness with the night that was not there while the sun was overhead. Perhaps it had something to do with being a predator, and unconsciously wanting the concealment of the shadows to cover one's comings and goings. I really could not tell you. Ultimately, it was not that I could not travel during the day, but rather that I chose to travel when I was more comfortable doing so. On the rare times when I encountered a human being at night during my travels, he or she most often was not up to anything good, thus, if I felt it necessary, I did not have to worry about feeding upon an innocent.

Yes, at this point in my existence, I had already determined to feed upon the criminal element if I at all had any kind of a choice. I thought of the people I had known who had run away rather than endure the siege any longer, and wanted to minimize the chance I would do something I might come to regret. Of course, over the centuries, I have discovered that this desire does not always have a base in reality. When one needs to feed, one feeds, and oftentimes, as there are hard and fast rules about feeding, there is not really a choice in the matter. Vampires are not caged reptiles to subsist upon the equivalent of prekilled, frozen food, and if you try to avoid the inevitable for too long, the choice will be taken from you and you will do it mindlessly.

It was my second feeding after I left the castle. I was ravenously hungry, but all there was nearby that could sustain me was an itinerant wood peddler who eked out his existence, as well as his wife's, on the outskirts of a stand of trees. I knew that they were happy together, and had no desire to destroy that sense of serenity in any way. Thus, invoking massive willpower and restraint, I hunted elsewhere, eventually finding a body, freshly dead and still slightly warm and only a little wolf-chewed. The other predator must have run off to a safer vantage point when it smelled me coming near. The remains were not pretty, but I determined to sustain myself on this unexpected prize, rather than to hunt a living human.

Ignoring the scent of death as much as I was able, I tore a hole in the throat of the corpse, and upended it like a nearly empty bag of broken sweets, sucking hard to pull in as much blood as possible. The blood had that odd taste that it developed when a person was about to die, only stronger, somehow, but I kept going until I could ingest no more. I then dropped the body and prepared to leave, proud of myself that I had discovered an alternate means of feeding. I would not have to find living humans to feed upon after all.

However, my relief was ill-considered and short lived.

At first, it was the barest trickle, and then I discovered that I was drenched in stinking rotting blood. I tore off my clothing and saw that blood was oozing out of my pores from my head to my toes. My pores had actually become larger in order to allow my body to reject all that blood. I must have looked like some ghastly demon standing there, blooding oozing and dripping from my every surface. It was not even a slow ooze, but in fact seemed to be fairly fast, as though my body was rejecting what I had tried to use to sustain myself. I tried to think of what could be causing this terrible reaction and then a particular seemingly innocent memory surfaced and the truth hit me:

When I had drunk Mathúin's water from his bowl shortly as I awakened from my death, I thought I had been hit with a massive attack of perspiration, however, even then, my body had rejected something it was unable to use. I would have thought that if my body could not digest something, I would throw it up as had happened while I was still human after eating bad meat. However, there must have been something else about me that had changed. Something new that was on an even deeper physical level than I realized. There was, it seemed, something particular to the blood from a living human that limited my feeding options. So much for trying to avoid the inevitable, I suppose. I would need to feed from living humans to survive.

I wandered until I found a small stream, and then washed my clothing and then myself, free of the clotted blood. I scrubbed hard at my hair to clear all the blood from its strands. The blood seemed to cling to it especially well, and it felt as though I could not scrub enough to rid myself of its stench. Tears stung my eyes with the pain of my fingernails digging at my scalp to remove all of that dead and stinking blood.

At that moment it all became too much and I sat down in the water. I began to cry in great, wracking sobs, mourning for myself and for the normal human life I would never have again. My new life, it seemed, was all about blood. Would my existence be filled with a cycle of feeding and endless scrubbing away of whatever spilled upon me in the course of filling myself up once more? I mourned the people who had died in the attack, even those with whom I had not gotten along or even disliked. No one deserved to die the way they had. They should have been given the chance to live and not be penalized for being in the wrong place at the wrong time.

It seemed that I had taken several baths in the past few days, but I could never seem to stay clean. From living with just a precious few baths in an entire lifetime to three in twice as many days further set my known universe on its undead ear. I sobbed for what seemed hours, letting the water take my watery red tears downstream as I allowed myself to cry it all out. When the crying finally calmed, I stood to face Mathúin, who had remained on the bank, waiting for me.

Mathúin had stayed away from me while I was still covered in old dead blood, as apparently, even he had more sense than I in this instance. Only once I had washed away the evidence of my poor feeding choice and returned to dry land did he deign to approach me to lick the droplets of water from my feet. I stared down at him as he offered this small act of devotion, and thought of what this four legged companion meant to me in a dangerous world where I was otherwise alone.

I had determined that periodically allowing him to lap up some of my own blood, such as it was, kept him as youthful and energetic as I had found him upon my first day of my new and unnatural existence. Indeed, he gamboled about as though he were once again a puppy, but when I called him to heel, he came with a speed and attention most unlike he had ever shown while I was still amongst the ranks of the human race.

There was some mental connection between us, Mathúin and me, and my summonses to him were not always verbal. There had already been several times when I had called him to me with a mental shout. When I was amongst the humans in non-threatening situations, I did what I could to avoid calling any more attention to my differences than was necessary, so at those times, I would use my voice. Nevertheless, when I did not have to pretend, it was wonderful.

Dawn was giving her maiden blush to the horizon, so I decided to leave my clothing on some nearby mossless boulders to dry while I climbed a tree, nestling in a conveniently arranged bough to sleep. The leaves and smaller branches of the tree made an effective blind to protect me from casual eyes, and my canine guardian would deal with the most tenacious offenders. There was no way that I would invite unwanted attention by sleeping naked upon the ground. Mathúin took up his place to guard me, and all was well with the world, thus I fell into my familiarly dreamless sleep, knowing that Mathúin would keep me safe.

I woke to the sound of his growling and the staccato clatter of hoofs nervously dancing on rock. Mathúin's growl was a truly terrifying sound, and with the flashes I got from him, this was a threat to be taken seriously. There was continued rustling and shrill whinnying down below as of a horse being roughly forced into low hanging branches, causing the tree to shudder, and Mathúin's growl became a bloodcurdling snarl. About to jump down to see what could possibly be causing such an outlandish disturbance, I caught an oddly familiar scent, though at that moment I could not have told you why it was so, but soon enough my curiosity would be satisfied.

"Who is there?" I demanded to know. My voice sounded harsh, even to my ears. "I warn you, do not come any closer, as I am well able to defend myself!"

"Why, it is I, your Sire, child. Come down and let me see you," responded a voice that sounded as though it expected total and absolute obedience, but its owner would find himself unpleasantly surprised.

I knew that voice to the very core of my bones, though I had heard it only once before and in a very nearly immediate response to hearing it my fangs and talons burst forth, fury and pure hatred boiling within me. I jumped down in front of him and snarled, baring my fangs at him. His horse, already heaving from a hard run and covered in lather, screamed in terror and reared, nearly unseating him, but he managed to remain mounted. He wore different clothing than he had been at the time of our first meeting. It made him look like a dandy. I suspect it was all that remained of a prior victim. His long, unblemished and deathly pale throat was framed by the froth of white lace, which lined the neckline of his blouse, which was enclosed within a red quilted vest. The pants he wore appeared to be of black leather, which was finished with matching riding boots and what appeared to be silver or steel spurs.

"I went back to the castle and saw your work. I knew I had to find you and bring you home. The big open world is no place for you, child," he told me.

"Leave me alone! I am no child and I want nothing to do with you!"

He laughed.

"I have given you a gift, child, a gift given to only a few lucky souls. I would think you would be grateful."

"You think that you have given me a gift? This is no gift. It is a curse! In one stroke, you have separated me from the human race! Why should anyone consider that to be a gift?" I cried in shocked and furious disbelief. The creature shook his head disdainfully and brushed twigs and shredded greenery from the front of his coat with a sour expression that I knew was not aimed at the flora he had knocked away.

"You are so much better than a mere mortal human, child, but even though you are a superior being, still you must be obedient to your Sire. That is the way things are. I am called Andreas, and I am your Master." he chided me with his thick German accent, swinging down from his huge dark gelding and staring into my eyes as though trying to force his will upon me. His mount rolled wild eyes at Mathúin and kept trying to break free as Andreas cruelly jerked the reins downward, drops of musky-smelling equine blood beginning to show in the lather at the corners of it is mouth. "Women, even nosferatu women, are not capable of being on their own! The philosopher Aristotle makes this clear. Females haven't the intellect."

"Is that what I am? This nost...nosf..."

"Nosferatu," he supplied in an infuriatingly offhand manner, his pronunciation of the word practically swallowing the final vowel so it was rendered as though the word ended with a somewhat breathy 't' sound instead of the final 'u' it possessed. "Some call us vampires. Now, come, child. I will not tolerate your dawdling, and you are to call me Master Andreas."

I found his rather snobbishly superior and assumptive attitude intolerable, especially after several days of successfully being on my own. How dare this popinjay try to tell me what to do?!

"I am obedient to none but myself, Andreas. This Aristotle of yours can go hang. Go on your way!"

He looked at me, chuckled softly and shook his head. He seemed not to be taking me very seriously at all and it was pissing me off. I stepped in close and stood on my toes to glare right into his eyes, hissing at him.

"Will you pit yourself against me, child?" he asked, almost sadly, making as if to turn away, mount his gelding and ride off in search of easier prey.

I felt myself begin to relax just the smallest bit and then, as though he could feel my wariness lessen and giving a toothy grin and shout of triumph, he let go the reins of his horse, spinning to face me and making as if to grab my arm. I cried out and raked his face with my talons, laying open the flesh of his cheek and leaving it hanging down to his earlobe. Clapping his hand to his ruined face, he staggered backward, nearly losing his footing. Regaining his balance, he snarled in fury and leapt at me once more, my impending murder flashing in his eyes.

Mathúin chose that moment to leap forward, barking wildly and slavering, ultimately latching his massive jaws onto Andreas' pale and unwisely exposed throat. Standing on his rear legs, he was so tall that he actually had to angle his head downward to get a firm grasp of that undead neck. The other vampire immediately forgot about me and began to try to fight off the enraged wolfhound. His surprising and impossibly high-pitched scream was cut off as Mathúin took a better hold of his throat, but he kept trying to rip the dog off him. Indeed, he tore great gashes in Mathúin's hide, but my guardian never faltered. This battle went on for several minutes, during which time the poor horse wisely put at least a few miles between itself and the three predators that terrified it.

Finally, the other vampire begged for my help.

"Get him off of me and I will leave you!" he cried. "Just make him stand down!"

I considered this for a few minutes longer, enjoying the sound of his screams, before coming to a decision. Somehow, I forced my will through Mathúin's rage and he let go of Andreas, but not before giving him a mighty shake that I could hear cracking bone. Andreas lay on his back beneath the heaving body of the sturdy wolfhound and stayed very still indeed. I could see that the vampire's eyes were open, and his mouth worked to say something that finally emerged as the barest of whispers.

"Please. Make him move. I swear that I will not touch you." he appeared to be much chastened now, but after his previous attempt at deception I suspected that this purported submission on his part was merely for show and that he merely sought another opening to attack me. Something deep within me screamed at me to let Mathúin finish the job and tear this Andreas apart, but another part of me refused to heed that voice and instead I heard myself verbally tell Mathúin to move away. The dog gave me a look I could not translate, but he obeyed me, snarling and growling all the while. I knew what his opinion was on the subject. There was no question about that.

Andreas picked himself up off the ground and went through the motions of dusting himself off. I could see the wound on his neck was already closing up, leaving no scar behind, much like what had happened to me when the castle thief had stabbed me with his dirk. The flesh of his cheek, however, had been completely torn away in his battle with the dog, revealing bone and desiccated looking muscle. For some reason, it appeared to be taking longer to heal than the throat wound. He tried approaching me once more, hand out in a much less threatening gesture, but Mathúin leapt between us, growling again, clearly unwilling to allow another attempted attack.

The vampire took a step back and hissed at the dog, perhaps trying to intimidate him. Mathúin only growled even more threateningly and showed his mouthful of sharp and very healthy teeth, at which point the vampire closed his own mouth, covering his fangs, trying to appear less of a direct threat. Mathúin sat on his haunches and continued his yellow-eyed stare at Andreas. He would not allow himself to be fooled again, and was letting the other vampire know this.

"You do not know what you are doing, child. You may be an adult woman, however, you are but an infant nosferatu. You need teaching. Come with me, and I will give you that instruction." he suggested, trying for what he likely thought was a reasonable suggestion in order to entice me to accompany him. He was not the first male to try to lure me into the stable, so I knew better. I watched him watching me expectantly, and so I took a moment to collect myself before responding. I was still angry, of course, but I needed to rein in that fury in order that I could think clearly, which was not at all easy under the circumstances.

"Andreas," I said through clenched teeth, "perhaps there may come a time when I would seek out your company, but now is not that time. I have had to look out for myself for many years now. I do not know if you know how life goes for someone like me, but I was never a sheltered child and once I became a woman, it was even more difficult for me. I have had to learn to look out for myself, and also know how to be discreet."

"My child..."

"Please stop calling me that! While you may be my...Sire...I believe you called it, I am not your child. I am called Siofra, so you may call me that, if you must call me anything at all!"

"Siofra, then. My dear Siofra, you really do not understand what it is to be a vampire. It is not like being human. As you probably already know, nosferatu look similar to the humans, but exotic enough to aid us in the hunt. They seem to find us fascinating. Perhaps there is something about us that draws them in as the scent of their blood and the sounds of their hearts draw us." I found it odd that he had gone from trying to force me to come along to being conversational, but continued to keep my guard up. He chose that moment to take my clothing from the boulder and hand it to me.

"For instance, you forgot, I am sure, that you were naked. You cannot be that forgetful amongst the humans, Siofra. They will take it badly and may attempt to lock you up." He gestured for me to put my clothes on, which I did post-haste, after unsuccessfully blushing. Vampires cannot blush. We do not, after all, use our veins to transport the blood we drink. I sat on a nearby boulder, combing my hair out before braiding it, as he continued.

"If you come with me, I will teach you how to be nosferatu. I offer you shelter while you pass through your infancy and childhood."

I tied my braid with a strip of leather and tucked it under my cap before I responded, the rictus of a pleasant smile pasted to my face much like the comedy mask of the classic Comedy and Tragedy symbols.

"I appreciate your *kind* offer, Andreas; however I prefer to go out on my own. Perhaps at some later date, I will seek you out and we can discuss our respective adventures, but for now, that is not something I want to do." I believe I sounded calm and sensible when I said it. Andreas, however, took it poorly.

"You do not know what you want or need! You are only a woman!" he sputtered at me, suddenly appearing to forget that he was trying to wheedle me into complacency. "Women must be sheltered and cared for; they are unable to do so for themselves."

"You do not seem to understand, Andreas, I do not want or need to be under your care. I am wise enough to make decisions for myself and will not tolerate your further interference. Leave me and go your own way, as I will go mine. I will be listening and watching for you, so do not think to take me unawares!" As I turned away, I heard a whisper of movement behind me, followed by a chilling snarl and a snap and then another high-pitched scream as Andreas whirled around to flee from a pursuing Mathúin and his large mouthful of very sharp teeth... I could hear him screaming my name as he ran, once again begging for me to call off my guardian, but this time, I let him run. I had no reason to pity him.

Not trusting Andreas to keep moving in the opposite direction from my own any longer than he must, I made my escape quickly, knowing that Mathúin would catch up to me once he had chased the other vampire far enough. I suspected that I would run into Andreas again. He seemed reluctant to allow me to make my own way. With his archaic attitudes, even for the time in which I lived, I suspected he was fairly old. He appeared not to consider the widowed grannies, midwives and hedge witches who lived on their own quite successfully. Surely they were not invisible to his vampire eyes, no matter how much he might want to make that so. Selective blindness exists, even in modern times.

It was a bit past dusk, so I was able to move quickly using my wildly enhanced speed rather freely, with little chance of being spotted by the local humans. The feeling of sheer freedom this gave me was truly exhilarating and I reveled in my newfound strength. It seemed my feet barely touched the ground as I ran, and I even managed to outrun the started deer and rabbits who startled and fled at my passing. They saw me as a predator and reacted appropriately, as they did not know that at least from me, they were actually safe. Venison simply did not have the allure it may have had in the recent past. Non-humans no longer struck me as being a potential food source, I did not even reminisce over the thought of the meals of my human past. It was as if I had never before eaten solid food, so I had no taste for it. To top it all off, animal blood even smelled wrong, and after the debacle of the previous day, I had no desire whatsoever to repeat the experience of my body rejecting what I consumed.

I covered some thirty miles or more in about an hour's time before I slowed to give Mathúin a chance to catch up a bit. In my mind, I could feel him tiring and did not have the heart to torture him further. While he was now much stronger than he had been before he tasted my blood and became more bound to me than ever he had been in the past, still he was not immortal.

I had been smart and removed my boots before starting my run, as I knew my boots, being already quite worn, would not be enough to tolerate the abuse they would have gotten as I nearly flew across the countryside. One thing I had not considered, however, was that the talons on my feet would emerge as I allowed myself to run unfettered. They tore into the rocky soil to provide better traction as I put a healthy distance between myself and my maker. Thus, even if my boots' thin soles had survived the run, my talons would have torn their toe boxes to shreds.

My hunger began to grow, and I realized that exerting so very much energy increased the chance that I would have to feed more frequently. Of course, my misadventure of the previous day meant that I was overdue to feed, so this only made it worse.

I found myself sniffing the wind, searching the breeze for the scent of likely prey. I scented a small gathering of humans, but instinct cautioned me against entering a situation already outnumbered, even if I could very likely overpower them all. Much like a pack of wild dogs will instinctively search out stragglers for their meals, my vampire instincts told me that this would be my best tactic for a successful hunt. It did not take long for me to locate my target.

She was huddled against a group of rocks, trying to conceal herself, though I knew exactly where she hid, as her body's natural warmth and the stench of the dead blood that had caked on her skin stood out to me like a candle's flame in a darkened room. She was a little thing who was even shorter than I.

I could tell that she had not yet heard my approach, but knew that might change at any time as I crept closer. It was only when I was about thirty feet away that I was also able to smell the musky stink of male seed on her clothing and skin. When I was about ten feet away and could catch the scent of her tears, I knew.

Rape. That small group I had avoided was a gang of brigands who had not been above taking their pleasure on the body of this mere child. A monstrous surge of anger rocked me and I involuntarily growled, causing the young girl to flinch and try to make herself an even smaller target against the rock. It sickened me.

Abandoning caution and forgetting that I now appeared much less than human, I stood up straight and made for her hiding place. I heard her muffled scream, the sound of her clapping a hand over her mouth and the frantic beating of her heart. As far as she knew, her tormentors had found her once again and may be intending to do away with her.

"It is all right," I told her when I was about five feet from her. I hunkered down and wrapped my arms around my knees, deliberately making myself appear much smaller and thus less of a threat. "I will not hurt you."

I could tell that she could not make out my features clearly, but I suppose she got enough detail in the dim light to be frightened about the monster before her. I imagine I must have appeared to be some pale-skinned ivory-fanged and monstrously taloned succubus, and it must have confused her that I had not yet attacked. I saw her pull a crucifix from under her nightshirt and fought to keep from laughing. She seemed to think I was some demon that needed banishing.

"Hold that out if you must, girl. I already told you that I intend you no harm. Please tell me what happened, though I can smell it on you, I think." I tried to sound reassuring, but my rage brought out an edge to my voice that even I could hear. My fangs were also fully extended in my mouth, so they tended to interfere with my speaking voice. I am sure that the combination of my appearance and the sound of my voice made quite the impression on an already terrorized and hysterical young woman.

After a few moments during which she must have been screwing up her courage, out poured a story that infuriated me even further, if such a thing were possible. It seems that the brigands had invaded her family's small cot about a league away, killed her elderly mother and two younger brothers, then had looted the place of what few valuables it possessed and then taken turns with the girl, who identified herself to me as Mary. She was a Catholic, then. Once they had spent themselves on her, they bound her hand and foot, and then drank themselves insensate. When she was sure that they all slept, she managed to wriggle free of her bonds and ran into the forest, not stopping until long after she was unable to hear the sounds of the camp behind her. At some point during her flight it became entirely too dark to travel, so she had stopped at the first reasonable hiding place, this was where I had found her.

I very nearly went to embrace her in consolation, however my instinct to feed was very strong and I did not want to do something I might later regret. I also knew that such an attempt would not be welcomed, but rather might throw her completely over the edge and into the depths of insanity. I strengthened my resolve not to feed on her by reminding myself that the group I had passed was now to be considered prime candidates for what I needed to do.

"Stay here and be safe until morning, then clean yourself up and find someone to help you and perhaps take you in. The brigands will not be troubling anyone any longer," I told her as I stood to leave. "How many of them were there?"

"I'm not sure. Four or five, I think. Probably only four. There was a dog there, too. What are you going to do?" she sniffled and wiped her nose with the edge of her tattered and dirty apron. The moon spilled through a hole in the clouds overhead to reveal a head of long yellow hair and a mouth a bit too wide for her face. A bruised left eye and swollen cheek marred what could have been a sweet kind of beauty.

The unexpected moonlight also revealed me to her, without shadows to conceal the worst of things.

She gasped and took an involuntary step backward at the sight of my true form, but to her credit, I saw her screw up her courage and take three long steps forward so she was only about three feet from where I stood. I had to appreciate her determination. I do not know if I would have been half so brave in her place. I smiled at her, working to keep my expression friendly, rather than a grimace.

"I will be visiting their camp and having a...discussion...with them. Don't worry about them any longer. They will no longer be a worry for you. Farewell," I said, and took off into the night, in the direction of the brigands' camp, my hunger adding even more of a spring to my step.

I heard her murmured farewell behind me, and knew I was doing the right thing.

Chapter Seven

When I arrived just outside their camp, I heard snoring that came from at least two people and someone who sounded as if he was coughing up a lung, but it appeared as though even the lookout had passed out from heavy alcohol consumption. Upon closer inspection, I saw that the young woman had been correct; there were four men spread about the rude camp in various examples of drunken disarray. Empty jugs and skins littered the ground, and the bones of what may have been either rabbits or chickens were flung around the campsite in a random fashion. The one wakeful creature in evidence, the camp's dog, was a scrawny and scabby looking but otherwise nondescript cur that, when he first saw me, began to lift its lips in a silent snarl, which I instinctively returned. At that point, the dog quickly averted its eyes from my own, instantly submissive as it recognized me as a superior predator.

I made a quick summoning gesture at the animal with my hand, though I was not sure of the response I would receive. I was quite surprised when the dog quite literally crawled on its belly all the way across the camp, coming to a stop in front of me, where it rolled onto its boney back, exposing its vulnerable and flea-ridden underbelly and throat to my pleasure, whatever that might be. Honestly, I found the entire display to be rather sad, but even though he obviously belonged to the brigands, I did not have it in me to kill the poor thing. I quickly squatted and rubbed my hand across his stomach, then pushed him away from me, pointing at the forest that loomed behind us. Apparently, even to the dog, my meaning was clear. He got to his feet, gave the tips of my fingers a single quick lick of what seemed to be gratitude, then slunk off into the dark though probably much less threatening shadows of the forest to meet whatever fate awaited him.

Once he was safely gone, I turned my full attention to the slumbering, sodden and sated two-legged curs before me. Instead of simply wildly rushing in, I surveyed the camp, looking for my best plan of attack. This entire scenario was completely new to me, and I didn't want to screw it up. However, there appeared to be some instinctive part of my new predator aspect that seemed happy to provide suggestions. So, after several minutes spent running those suggestions around in my mind, I decided on the one that seemed to make the most sense. It promised the best chance of doing as much damage as possible before anyone would be able to attempt to defend the camp.

I started with the sentry, a skinny pock-marked young man of perhaps sixteen years, clad in a dirty homespun tunic and heavily stained leather pants. It was a shame that one so young would have fallen in with such a group, but if he was old enough to make such a decision, he was old enough to face the consequences of his foolishness. Grabbing him so quickly that he was unable to sound an alarm, I clamped a hand over his mouth and dragged him into the night. Once I was a couple hundred yards in, and far enough away from the camp that his muffled screams could not be heard by his compatriots, I used him to sate my deep hunger, after whispering into his ear about how vengeance would be had for what had occurred with that young woman I had discovered in the forest. How he was but the first of his ill-gotten friends to experience my particularly terrible brand of retribution and how very much I would enjoy it. He must have been lucid enough to understand me, even through his drunken fog, as he gave a high, thin squeal which I heard through the intervening barrier of my hand.

"You have made poor choices," I told him as I turned him so he could see my face. I smiled a smile that did not meet my eyes but showed my fangs in all their ivory glory. "Now you must pay the price for your mistakes. Not even the *bean sí* will mourn your passing."

SIOFRA

Eyes wide in terror and with muffled pleas for an undeserved mercy that would not be granted, he struggled to free himself from my grasp, but the alcohol left him far too uncoordinated to have any real success. Adventures such as those he had previously experienced were not supposed to end this way, I assume. I continued to whisper sweet inanities into his ear, my eagerness to feed becoming even more heightened and thrilling through me. Then the point came where I could resist no longer and I tore into his throbbing carotid artery. I roughly clamped my mouth over that gushing font to begin enthusiastically sucking his life away.

Once he passed out from massive blood loss, I pulled out a few more deep gulps, then broke his neck and dropped him to the ground, leaving his nearly bloodless remains to be eaten by wild animals. He was not worth even taking the time to throw a handful or two of dirt over his carcass, much less pausing to bury him. My need to feed had been satisfied, and I felt my strength returning, as well as an overall sense of what I suppose would be health on my part. If I had been able to see myself at that moment, I would have noted that the bones of my face were no longer as sharp and that the blood, which now suffused my flesh, had lent a dash of color to my cheeks. The creatures who called this forest home would have quite a feast before them, once I finished my work.

As I returned to the camp, I kept an ear open for the sounds of activity therein, but it seemed they remained asleep and completely unaware of their diminishing numbers. There was only the sound of steady snoring as the three fell more deeply to sleep. I had time to consider and plan my next attack.

My next target was someone who appeared to have performed cooking duties for the camp. Where the lookout had been a young man with greasy shoulder length dirty blonde hair pulled into a rude queue at the nape of his neck, this one appeared to be the oldest, with close-cropped dark hair that sported gray at his temples. His skin had the same sickly yellow hue that my previous household's chief groom had shown before he died a terrible wasting death. Indeed it was a shame that I could not leave this one to that selfsame fate, but who knew how long he might survive before the final darkness took him from this plane. Making my way to him, my nose finally picked up a scent of wrongness. Something more than filth and drink would create. I was getting my first scent of terminal illness in a human being, but did not realize it at the time. All I knew was that some part of my mind was telling me that this was not the best source for food. I did not yet know that his illness would not affect me, but this was my first inkling that my instincts would direct me toward healthy prey if given the chance.

He wore a foul-smelling blood and grease stained leather jerkin and some ill-fitting trousers that must have come from one of the group's previous raids. The dirt encrusted remains of a small mammal carcass were clutched in one of his hands, as though he had passed out mid-mouthful and dropped where he stood, a few feet from the burnt out fire pit. A flurry of wet sounding coughing from him identified him as the man who had broken the night's peace with the sound of his labored hacking.

Pausing a moment so I could listen more carefully, I was able to hear the sound of the fluid and mucous that had gathered in his lungs sloshing as he fought to inhale each breath of air. I could not help but wonder what creature or disease was devouring him from the inside.

I picked my way through loot that had been thrown carelessly about the camp as they studied their gleanings. Precious books were strewn across the ground and small pieces of jewelry and shiny religious objects were piled in a small area near the man I assumed to be the leader of the group. The leader was not yet my target as I approached the ostensible cook. Looking at the blood-flecked sputum that caked his cheek and chin, I felt a certain reluctance to even touch him, but I knew that I must if I wanted to end their depredations.

Coming in close and swiftly grabbing his head to drag him up off the ground in almost a single movement, I ground my hand a little too hard against his mouth as I took him, feeling one or two of his front teeth break as I dragged him a little apart from the rest of his unconscious band. His eyes flew open revealing whites that were nearly as yellow as his skin. A bare squeak made it past the iron of my hand as the teeth snapped in his mouth. As had his predecessor, he tried to fight me off. I did not give him the chance to get the better of me, as instead of dragging him off into the forest to feed upon, I simply twisted his head on his shoulders until I heard his spine snap and felt his body relax into death, then laid him gently back onto the ground. My gentleness had nothing to do with any depth of feeling, but was merely part of my desire to make as little noise as possible. The stench of his bowels cutting loose as he died was oddly satisfying to me as I decided upon my next target.

I had quickly dispatched the first two, who were both still so drunk that they were on the verge of alcohol poisoning, but I could see from their terrified expressions that they were all too aware of their fate. The gods help me, I must admit that watching the light go out of their pleading eyes made me smile. Who knew how many people they had killed in the time since they had started their journey down the road they had chosen to travel in life? I was not about to let that brutality continue any longer. Yes, this was only one band, but I had already decided that I would do my part to thin out their numbers as often as possible.

In those days, I was still a fool.

Those newly born to blood often make these kinds of promises when they do not yet truly understand the limitations placed upon them by their transformation. Once they realize that their own self-destruction is not going to happen, fledgling vampires really do believe they can eke out an existence feeding only on thieves and cutthroats. They just do not yet understand that one cannot stick to noble ideas such as these forever. Even if you are daily elbow to elbow with those upon whom you plan to feed, you still must find those opportunities to hunt discreetly. Fate is not necessarily going to give you carte blanche on when you may hunt. You feed when the opportunity strikes, as trying to stretch out intervals between feedings, even for the best of reasons, can and do end very badly.

Right now, I felt myself to be a crusader of sorts, ridding the world of monsters such as these. I did not yet know that over the subsequent four hundred plus years, there would be times when someone in the wrong place at the wrong time ended up assuaging my hunger. It would not matter that the next day I would come upon a cellar full of slumbering opium addicts. I fed when I was able to do so.

Now I had removed half of their number and all that remained were the last two members of the band. These two lay near one another, and had likely either fallen asleep or passed out mid-conversation. Their positions near one another suggested something closer to friendship than a business relationship. The others has been members of the band, but were not part of the "family". A closer look and recognition of facial similarities between these last two made me realize they were actually related to one another. Was this a family business after all?

I really had to think this part of the attack through, as I was concerned that whomever I grabbed first might kick out at the other and waken him at an inopportune time for me, so it was important that I plan carefully. The first two had been ridiculously easy to dispatch, compared to what this last pair promised to be. It was unlikely that it would all be so simple to accomplish.

I eased my way through the litter of their celebration and bent over one of them, trying to angle myself in the best way to grab the man as silently as possible. Sadly, the Fates had other plans, as I soon discovered. While I imagined myself the hand of Justice and all that, they apparently felt that I had to prove myself worthy or some such.

Bitches.

All hell broke loose as I grabbed the smaller of the two remaining human-shaped beasts and failed to get my hand over his mouth in time to prevent an outcry. He shouted out a crude epithet, causing his one last living friend to shudder into wakefulness. The man grabbed his knife up in his right hand, and hefted a stout cudgel in the other. His eyes never left mine as he rose unsteadily to face me. Drunk he may have been, but he was experienced enough to know his business in a fight. Perhaps some of his intoxication was relieved by the adrenaline that now coursed through his body.

This last man, whom I had decided earlier was their leader, assumed a stance that suggested he was well accustomed to hand to hand combat. He held the knife with a practiced ease, holding it so that it was below his wrist, blade facing outward and ready for him to slash at me with it. He took a step toward me as though I had divined his intent. When he yelled some challenge at me, I was unable to understand a word of what he said, but his tone of voice and his stance screamed threat in any language and likely included a demand that I release my captive.

Knowing I would have trouble battling the two of them at once, I threw my current captive into the nearest oak, hearing a satisfying crunch as several of his bones, including his skull, shattered upon contact with the hard wooden bough of the venerable tree. A few acorns fell to the ground, knocked loose from the impact, so hard had I thrown him.

My opponent watched his friend fly through the air and gave out a tragic cry as the man impacted the tree. I wondered if this was some relative of his, but quickly dismissed this line of thought as irrelevant. I never took my eyes from the last man, but my peripheral vision caught faint movement from the unfortunate fellow beneath the tree as he ineffectually tried to crawl away, blood pouring from several puncture wounds gained from his ill-fated congress with the tree. Fortunately, having fed fully earlier, the salty sweet bounty spilling out onto and soaking into the ground did not distract me.

That was fine, as far as I concerned. They would soon be able to have a long discussion about what had just happened to them once they reached whatever afterlife awaited them. I drew in a deep breath and glared at him.

"You really thought that you could slaughter an old woman and her little boys, and then take turns raping the lone child you deigned to allow to live and believe there would be no repercussions? How many others have you raped and murdered over the years? This is not something you could have gotten away with forever. You were a very stupid man to even think that would be possible," I chided him quietly, shaking my head. "There is always payment due for one's actions, good or bad, although sometimes it may take awhile for it to finally find you. But it does, in the end...and this time, I am that end."

Three breaths were required to get all of that out. I was going to have to learn how to speak all over again so that my words did not come out sounding stilted. Perhaps I should practice verbal economy whenever I had the opportunity.

He did not seem to accept my conclusion for some unfathomable reason. Had he missed the fresh carnage around him? It should have caught his attention almost immediately that a seemingly tiny and helpless woman had killed his compatriots. It was time to shake up his narrow worldview and see what happened then.

"I rape you next!" he shouted in broken Gaelic, spit spraying from his mouth, showing gaps and the remains of broken and rotting teeth. I could smell his stinking breath from five yards away. How surprising. "You will scream love for me before I kill you!"

"I really doubt that," I responded, as quietly as I had earlier spoken. My rage boiled within me like a pressure cooker on steroids. I smiled at him, this time showing him my fangs. "If someone is getting raped, it's going to be you, *fool*."

"Vampire *bitseach*!" he shrieked, his eyes widening in horror. Now *those* were words I understood. He fumbled in his shirt and pulled out a metal crucifix on a chain, thrusting it out in front of him as though he believed it would have some power over me. A part of me wondered from whom it had been stolen, as I doubted it had originally belonged to him.

I laughed, which seemed to confuse him, and he shifted his glance to the crucifix, as though he wondered if he was brandishing the correct object, whatever that might be. These religious types often seemed to feel as though their faith had more power than any other, but I was an atheist, so perhaps that was why none of them had any control over me.

"Is that supposed to mean something to me? I mean, it is oddly pretty, but really. Wearing the image of an executed man? That's fairly disgusting, even to me. Your dog has left you, by the way. It apparently felt no need to protect you. Perhaps you disgusted it as well." I really needed to learn to control my words. I was discovering that vampires are creatures of impulse and strong emotion. Something like that could end up coming out badly. Like right now.

As if in answer, he rushed me, slashing wildly with his knife and swinging his cudgel at my head. I felt the blade slash through my blouse and into my gut, the pain like a hot brand across my midsection. Ignoring the pain as best I could, I darted in and knocked the cudgel out of his hand and across the camp, leaving my opponent with just the knife. Knowing I was fighting for my life, such as it was, I kept out of reach of the shining blade, hoping to tire out my target while he did his level best to try to end me. I taunted him as we danced, hoping to goad him into a thoughtless mis-step. The pain in my gut did not ease, feeling rather raw and more than a little tender.

"Did it require all of you to hold down a defenseless girl while you took turns stealing her maidenhead? Was she too strong for you?" He responded with unintelligible cursing in whatever his native tongue might be. To me, it all sounded like so much drunken nonsense. "Were you even able to get your release, or are you the one she called 'Little Prick' who could not even stick it inside her?"

I must have learned to control myself eventually, because I am telling you my story, but at this particular moment in time...

He must have understood far more of what I said than I thought he was able. Never mistake a thick accent for an inability to understand what is being said, Siofra. The man, now frothing with rage, rushed at me, screaming. When I did not move away quickly enough, he stabbed the knife point-first deep into my chest, with so much force that the blade ground against bone and sent shooting pain throughout my body. He then twisted the blade inside me and I fell to my knees, screaming in agony. The man took that opportunity to run into the forest as fast as he could, obviously hoping to escape me. Call it an early lesson in not being overconfident.

It took me a few minutes to get hold of myself and be able to focus on the situation at hand. Once you have started screaming, it is sometimes hard to stop. The knife protruded from my chest all the way down to the hilt. If it had not been I impaling me, I might have been able to appreciate its artisanship and beauty. As it was, I simply wanted it gone from my body.

I took hold of the hilt with my right hand and tried to pull it out of my chest, but found I was unable to do so, as it appeared that it was wedged against at least one of my ribs. I was surprised to see only a little blood staining my shirt, but certainly not anything like one would expect from a chest and gut wound. I then grabbed the knife's hilt in both hands and yanked outward, screaming with pain as the knife once again ground past bone and finally slid out of my body. The blade was practically clean when I looked at it, but I could plainly see that a piece of the point perhaps the length of the first joint of my finger had broken while it was inside me. Not good. I had no idea how I would dig it out, or even if I could.

SIOFRA

A quick look at my chest and gentle prodding at the wound showed that my flesh was not what it once had been. It reminded me of something called a *sponge* I had seen amongst the toiletries of one of our wealthier lady guests. Her maid had told me it was all that remained of some sort of sea monster. She had showed me how it could gather up water within itself, which could then be squeezed back out again. I had found it to be nothing short of miraculous and determined that if the opportunity ever presented itself, I would purchase one for my own use.

The gut wound he had given me earlier in our battle exposed a tangle of innards in my abdomen that must have been my intestines, but they appeared to be empty, which shocked me. I was also surprised that the two wounds had not healed up immediately, as had my previous injuries, but something told me that kind of seemingly miraculous healing probably required something else to initiate the process. I could feel it teasing me, as though I should know what it was, but I was unable to grab hold of that wisp.

I did not have time to investigate more fully, as my quarry was attempting to escape by concealing himself in the forest. I could still hear his footfalls as he blundered through the darkness. In addition to my original reason for wanting him dead, I was also angry that he had damaged not only me, but my blouse as well. It was not as though I had a handy wardrobe with fresh clothing available.

I went into the forest after him, tracking him by both the musky scent of his unwashed body and the sounds of his desperate and panicked flight. I did not bother to rush. His eyesight was not anywhere near as keen as mine under the densely clustered trees. I heard the thud of an impact and his muffled gasp of pain as he blundered over a root or a downed branch. He must have done himself a little bit of damage when he fell, as his gait changed to something more lumbering and I could suddenly scent the enticing aroma of his blood on the breeze. I kept after him, calling out to him every so often to remind him that I had not given up my pursuit, though I dragged things out a bit. I wanted him terrified and exhausted by the time I caught up with him. It would make him that much more careless when we resumed our fight.

I kept him moving for another hour or so before I tired of the chase, my hunger becoming more acute and on the verge of actually being painful, especially in the area of my still open wounds. Stepping up my pace, I quickly closed the distance between us.

I could hear him gasping and muttering under his breath in his own language. Perhaps he was praying. I have no idea. He was weaponless now, so I was a bit more brazen in my approach, confident that he was too hysterical to think clearly. The thunder of his heartbeat in my sensitive ears was as a trumpet to me in the forest, now that I stood so very close to him. I had spiced him just right, a vampire chef seasoning her upcoming meal.

"Well, hello again," I said as I stepped closely enough to him that he could easily see me. He started in shock, his eyes wide and staring. His heartbeat thudded in my ears like a frantic rapping at the door. I saw blood running down his right shin and trickling down into the dirt. That must have been the injury he suffered when he fell earlier. I felt a pang of sadness watching all that precious blood being wasted, unconsciously running the tip of my tongue across my upper lip in my excitement.

The man tried to muster some of his previous bravado, but fell far short. He swung his otherwise empty fists at me, but favoring his right leg and still under the influence of so much drink, miscalculated and fell forward into my arms like a swooning female. Pulling him in close to me, I drank deep of his scent, his terror perfuming the air more strongly than any aphrodisiac.

Well, with this one, I could feed a bit more leisurely and I would. He had not only injured me, he had led that gang of ruffians. To him belonged the worst retribution I could mete out.

"I guess I'll take my time with you, as you did with that young woman. She is still alive, by the way. So sorry to disappoint," I told him with patently false regret. He whimpered like a bereft puppy, with no succor or help in sight. "Your friends had quick deaths, compared to what yours will be."

I ran my tongue along his cheek and deliberately grazed his skin with a fang in the process. The dried blood there tasted nearly rotten to my sensitive tongue, but I had done it more for effect than anything else. It succeeded in its intent, leaving him sobbing and in hysterics, and causing him to foul himself as his bladder let go.

As he was the only one left at this point, I had no need to muffle his screams of agony and terror, which echoed long into the night as I killed him a sip at a time.

Chapter Eight

I discovered as I drank his life away that it seemed I required a fresh source of blood in order to heal my wounds. By the time I was finished, my gut was as good as new once more. It took a while, since I drank so slowly, but it was a very good lesson for me in what I needed to do in order to survive. Unfortunately, there remained a very small opening in my chest where the knife had entered, and a slight amount of dark fluid seeped slowly from it. I assumed that it was from the point of the knife that remained lodged in the bone. I wondered if I should worry about getting it out, but knew that short of cutting myself open and removing it myself, I was not going to be doing that any time soon. I left the body where it fell as the man died. I was deep enough into the dense forest that short of someone stumbling over the body, there was little chance he would be found before he was anything except for bones.

Before taking to my leafy perch the night before, I had returned to the camp and looted the bodies, carefully gathering up the items the bandits had so carelessly strewn about the area, including the illuminated manuscripts and other books. I tied them very carefully into a bundle, intending to give them all to the young woman when I found her again. They were not the bandits' to keep, or mine, either. Perhaps their return would give her some peace, if nothing else.

I slept out the day high up in the branches of a tree that was far enough away from any of the newly dead that I could not readily smell them. It was during this time that Mathúin returned from wherever he had broken off his chase of Andreas. He somehow found "my" tree and slept beneath it, waiting patiently for my own return to consciousness.

When I finally woke and climbed back down, he greeted me with wild enthusiasm. From the scent of blood and meat on his breath as he enthusiastically greeted me, it was obvious that he had fed on a deer at some time during his return to me. He sniffed at the hand that had petted the bandits' former dog and gave me a curious look as though asking what had happened. As we walked back to the camp, I explained what had transpired, not caring if he understood or not, but the act of speaking what I had done helped to calm my mind. I was surprised when we entered the wreckage of the camp and I double checked to be certain I had missed nothing, that Mathúin urinated all around it, clearly marking his territory and indicating his disdain for its former inhabitants.

I bathed myself and washed my bloodied and torn clothing in a nearby pond, not wanting to have the blood of my victims on me any longer than I must. I also did not want to go back to the young woman looking like some wild and terrible sí creature. In the light of day, I would look even more terrible than I had during the previous night. While I was in the water, I took the time to also watch Mathúin, as he was much in need of a good bath. His scent was rank and sharp on my very sensitive nose. While young Mary might not be able to smell him, I was more than able to do so and chose not to make things any worse for myself than they need be.

After getting myself cleaned up and getting everything together, including some reasonably clean clothing for Mary's use, I returned to where I had left her, but she was gone. I followed her scent and her tracks to the edge of a cliff about a quarter mile from the place I found her the night before. When I looked down, I saw her broken and bloodied body on the rocks below. I divined that in her despair, she had either wandered out blindly during the night and fallen to her death or had chosen to kill herself. Either way, her pain was ended. It was not my place to decide if her decision was good or bad, if she had indeed decided to end her life.

I was now the owner of a large bundle of ill-gotten but brutally recovered booty, although I chose to believe that their previous owners would not begrudge my possession of them, as the bandits who had taken them were now a thing of the past. I would use whatever money I could get for them to ease my travels as much as possible. Unlike I had with the brigands, I took the time to bury Mary, along with the crucifix I had taken from around the neck of the bandit leader. It seemed the kind and appropriate thing to do.

I encountered no one else before I arrived at Killarney, where I made one quick stop to order one particular item before going to arrange my next appointment. I received a few odd looks from the townsfolk, but kept my eyes forward as I sought out the tavern. It was an old building with relatively fresh straw thrown over moldy leavings on the floor. It did not smell particularly wonderful to me, but the locals were probably very used to it. I am sure that a good raking out and a completely fresh layer of straw would work wonders for the place, but that was not up to me.

A scrawny, pimply-faced and particularly brusque serving wench came to my table to demand my requirements and I so I ordered ale I had no intention of drinking whilst I waited for the local two legged rats to make their approach.

"You have to order something or you can't stay in here, woman," the barkeep called to me from behind his counter. "You cannot loiter here."

"She's wanting a pot of ale, William," the wench supplied in a nasal whine, to which the barkeep grunted and turned to draw a tankard of the stuff which he then laid on the counter for his girl to pick up, a chore accomplished in remarkably short order. He had probably been serving ale from the tap since he was a wee lad.

"Is she wanting a room, then?"

The wench looked at me.

"No. I'll be on my way after I complete my business," I called to the man. He gave a single nod of understanding and then went back to his duties behind the wooden bar. Obviously it did not matter one way or the other whether or not I stayed.

I unsuccessfully tried to fend off a wandering pig that came over to sniff at me, apparently not intimidated by my changed nature or my importuning to him to simply leave. I hadn't had much to do with them while I was alive, so this was a fairly new experience to me. After it thoroughly inspected my legs and boots, it chose to lie in the straw at my feet, where it very quickly fell asleep. I imagined that at some point, the pig would find itself on the menu. Allowing it to wander and beg for scraps while it was fairly young probably kept the overall feed bill down. I wondered at what point Piggy here would be wrestled into a regular hog pen while he continued to fatten up for nice thick slabs of bacon.

Wonderful. Just what I needed. Food with wanderlust.

After a few discreet inquiries and a small number of pennies spent for an equal number of fleet and eager young messengers, I found myself speaking with a local townsman who took all of the books off my hands if not for what they were actually worth on the legitimate market, then not too terribly far from that price. He was a fairly effeminate but immaculately dressed man who asked few questions of me, as though unwilling to discover how, exactly, I had acquired the volumes, but eager enough for them to not try haggling too hard in case I decided to take my merchandise elsewhere. The carefully rendered and colorful illuminations made them pretty to look at, even if you were unable to read the book itself, which was my own situation. The man seemed to be especially excited about a few that boasted gold foil in their illuminations, and he shoved a fat purse at me that lay surprisingly heavy in my hand. I made the purse disappear into the waist of my trousers, where others would be unable to detect it unless they came stupidly close to me.

"Are you certain you do not wish to spend a night or two at my townhouse?" he offered, though I could hear in his voice that he really had no desire to have me under his roof. He had come to meet me in the tavern after I declined his invitation to visit him at his home. He surreptitiously eyed the snoring pig at my feet as I pretended to nurse my tankard of ale. He was likely afraid that I would attempt to steal from him. He was blissfully unaware that should I accept his invitation, that it would be his life, not his possessions, that would be in grave danger. I hoped that the frequent hunger I experienced was more a symptom of my newness as a vampire, rather than something I would have for the rest of my existence. As it was, spending an extended period of time with mortal humans was not something I cared to do any time soon.

I declined as gracefully as I could.

"I am expected elsewhere this evening, though I thank you for your kind invitation. Perhaps you might give me leave to call on you should I return to Killarney in the future."

The man gave a jerky nod, mumbled an insincere affirmative, clutched his new leather-wrapped treasures to his chest, and waddled off down the street, a pair of burly manservants *cum* bodyguards in his wake. I wasn't any more interested in remaining in this town as he was in having me visit his home, and in fact would only remain only another hour or so before I moved onward. That should be just long enough to find something to eat.

In point of fact, it was not long before a drunken fool who smelled of pine tar and stale rum stumbled over to my table and propositioned me, throwing a few pennies onto the table's surface.

"'m lookin' fer a good screw, 'n you look like you'll do as good as any other," he stated, as though this should make me fall into whatever he called a bed. I wonder how often this had worked for him.

I looked up into his ugly face and smiled winsomely, my new aspect practically breathing sexuality and numbing him to any inkling of danger. His moth to my flame.

"Lead on, good sir," I breathed, heaving my bosom at him, rising gracefully and following him out the door after grabbing up the pennies from the tabletop. Money was money, and it all spent. I put my full tankard on the ground before the pig and gave it a final scratch across the top of its head. The pig opened its tiny black eyes to look at me, grunting its pleasure and perhaps a porcine farewell. He had not been a poor companion, after all.

It was all I could do not to attack the man at the instant we left the tavern. I was hungry and had already discovered that my being hungry could lead to serious mis-steps, which I did not care to repeat. Thus, I waited as the drunk led me to a dank, dirty shack in an unsavory part of town and beckoned me inside. It was dark, so he could not see my fangs, which had emerged in anticipation of the feeding to come. I, however, could see in the dark almost as well as I could during the day. The man gestured at his louse-ridden bed, fully expecting me to climb into it, which was most certainly not going to happen.

Instead, I reverted to my coquettish predator aspect and glided up close to him, putting one arm around his shoulders and cupping his cheek with the other, leaning forward to kiss him, careful to keep my lips between my fangs and his searching tongue. Clearly, he had not expected this, thinking me to be one of the local whores, and his body reacted almost instantly, his little soldier quickly coming to attention and saluting me.

He swore angrily at his body's betrayal, and tried to push me down onto his bed. I countered by planting my feet solidly so as to keep my balance. I murmured a remonstrance at him, but made it sound playful instead of angry. Whatever his opinion might be on the matter, I was the one in charge, so I would decide what would transpire. Oddly, as hungry as I was, I did not want it all to be over too soon, so I teased him a bit with my hands and my lips. I tugged gently at his belt, loosening it and then throwing it onto his bed. Once that was accomplished, I slowly worked his tunic over his shoulders and head to reveal a surprisingly hairy chest on a scrawny torso. I leaned forward and licked his nipples, which instantly caused them to come erect.

He groaned with his need, and I ran my tongue from his nipples, up his chest and to his throat, where I nibbled playfully. The hand I kept in the vicinity of his groin felt that area surging in response to my tender ministrations and I felt it when, excited beyond all thought, he climaxed.

As he prematurely spent himself in unexpected pleasure, staining his trousers with his diseased sperm, I moved in for the kill, plunging in my fangs, tearing his flesh and drinking deeply. The rise in blood pressure that I had deliberately caused in him with my curious foreplay helped to propel his blood into my mouth and down my eager throat. Timing my drinking to coincide with his heartbeat, I expended very little energy in obtaining my prize. He never even knew enough to put up any kind of a fight and died peacefully in my arms. I could taste some kind of taint in his blood, though not enough of one to make me reject it. Whatever it was that I tasted would probably have killed him within the next few months anyway, so I had only hastened his end and perhaps saved him future agonies.

He looked quite peaceful as I held him, no longer having a care in the world. Of course, I could not leave him to be discovered with the wound I had given him, so a plan was necessary to destroy the evidence of my having been there. I made a mental note that whenever possible, I should avoid feeding within populated areas.

First, I gathered all his personal possessions from around the room, which were not many at all, and then laid them all in his bed before putting him there as well, pulling the rotten blankets up over his chest. Then I lit the sole oil lantern in the place and knocked it over onto the rotten wood and cloth of the bed, which quickly caught fire. His body was slow to ignite, but once it did, the air quickly began to stink of burning and burned meat. I waited to leave the place until I saw that the bed was fully engulfed, and that there was no chance of the damage

I had done being discovered. I stepped out the door and into the cool night air. I was glad that due to my unique condition, smoke inhalation was not a consideration.

"Fire!" I yelled out, more to catch the attention of any who might live nearby and who might need to keep their own possessions safe from the fire. A few curious folk poked their heads out their doors and when they saw that it was in their best interest to respond, ran outside to try to put out the flames. I called out once or twice more, but by this time, the locals had set up their own cry, so I simply stood by to watch events unfold.

Once I was certain the flames were going to destroy any evidence of my presence, I quickly left the place, Mathúin emerging from where he had hidden just on the edges of Killarney and we disappeared into the welcoming embrace of the night.

Chapter Nine

After having sold the rather exotic books in the tavern, I had no desire to tempt the local thieves any more than necessary. I had noted one or two seedy looking characters who seemed overly curious about my business and possessions. Keeping this in mind, my plan was to return to town in the morning to collect what I had ordered from a local merchant who was more than willing to work through the night for what I needed from him.

That night, I rested in an old, abandoned stable a few miles from Killarney. Stripped of any portable hardware, the stable was a mere shell of what it once had been. Three of the four stone walls still stood, a great hole in one side loudly proclaiming the strength of Mother Nature: the remains of a great oak lay across the shattered stones as though a Scottish god or goddess had stopped by to participate in caber tossing. Only a single desiccated strip of old and cracked leather remained, threaded through a knot in one of the wooden studs that lined the walls. Even the hasps and hinges had been removed from the stall doors, any metal being something of at least some small value in this time and place.

In fact, it had been so long since any actual livestock had lived within its walls that any old remaining manure was dried out and almost powdery. An Irish barn owl, valentine-shaped white face and black eyes showing up brightly to my enhanced vision, roosted on the high center beam of the structure, not too terribly far from the bundle of twigs and feathers that was probably its nest. It hooted softly as it eyed me below, as though considering something. The owl's presence meant that no pigeons were in residence, either, so that was fine with me. Pigeon crap had never one of my favorite things.

"Hello there," I told the owl softly. "I'll just be passing the night here. I won't be staying."

The owl turned its head to regard me for a long moment with its unblinking stare, then hooted once more and flew off into the darkness on silent wings through one of many holes in the thatched roof, seeming to accept my terms. I was glad that it had not felt threatened by my presence.

I spent a quiet night in the barn, buried in a very old pile of straw and was able to rise the next morning feeling well rested and comfortable for the first time in a long while. The owl was back on its perch, and it opened its eyes when whatever noises I made caught its attention. I briskly saluted it in reply.

"Thanks for the night's lodging, friend owl. Good hunting to you!" I told it as I brushed straw from my hair and clothing.

It did not deign to reply as I slipped out the door of the stable and into the warm golden light of the sunrise. The air was cool, the only sound I could hear the first sounds of daylight living birds waking and starting their own days. I have loved this time of day as long as I can remember, as it is one of the few truly peaceful times of day.

Mathúin was off out of earshot chasing up something for his breakfast, which was fine with me, since I was not in any particular hurry. I took the opportunity of a leisurely walk back to town and used my nose to find my first errand of the day...

"So you be needing a good horse, eh, gel?" The liveryman eyed me up and down, as though taking my measure. "I got a mare here that'll do you a good trick!"

The livery stable was on the outskirts of town, with a corral full of horses and ponies of various quality and condition available to rent. None was anything I was interested in using, especially as I was looking to purchase my own mount. It turned out that the better mounts being offered for sale were housed in the long wood and stone building that served as the actual stable, so there I was, dickering with the owner and trying very hard not to lose my temper. The area was poorly lit, which was probably a tactic on the part of the owner to conceal the flaws of poor quality animals until money changed hands and the sale was final.

He started down the long aisle toward a stall, which contained a placid looking brown animal, but I stopped him with a quick hand laid atop his shoulder. She was pretty, but I was not looking for pretty.

"I need something a bit more sturdy and spirited, as well as the tack to ride it. I do not need or want a lady's palfrey, sir. I want an animal that will travel well over hard terrain and long distances. That one is more suited for slow and easy travel."

"A lady's palfrey is appropriate for you, woman. You are not of the right stature to possess something more...er...energetic," he protested.

"Well, that is not up to you, sir that is up to me. What do you have available for me to buy right now that will meet the needs I have previously stated?"

I was starting to lose my patience with the man, as we had been dancing this dance for nearly three quarters of an hour and I still had other errands to complete. The liveryman had started his maddening sales tactics by showing me an ancient nag that was experiencing such a difficult time standing on its own that it was actually leaning against the logs that made up the corral outside. I believe his top selling point had been the pathetic animal's coal black hide. I'm not sure why he had considered that to be a desirable attribute in a mount. At this time in its Methusalen life, its top selling point was that little flesh would need to be flensed from its bones once it met its final appointment at the knacker's. Perhaps the liveryman had thought me a foolish and impulsive female. It would not be the first time, or the last, that this would be thought of me.

"These are the only animals that I will consider selling to you, madam. You will not change my mind in this!"

"Let me make that decision. I have the coin to purchase what I wish." I fancied that his eyebrows moved higher on his forehead at this, as though he could not quite bring himself to believe what I said.

In the midst of our arguing, we were interrupted by a shrill whinny from a stall at the end of the dark aisle and I immediately began to make my way in that direction. The liveryman attempted to insert himself between my goal and me but I wordlessly shoved him aside and continued on my way. In my impatience, I must have pushed him a bit too hard, as he was thrown into one of the other stalls, which, fortunately for him, was empty. I did not particularly care either way for the man's safety and did not stop, continuing to walk down the stable aisle. Yes, he had managed to piss me off and I had had enough.

The sharp sound of hooves striking the side of the stall was a hollow staccato in the air, punctuated by yet another sharp whinny. By this time, I could see the animal's outline more clearly, but it was too dark for me to get much detail. I could dimly hear the liveryman shrieking at me to stay away as I walked up to the stall door and held out a hand to the frothing bundle of fury within.

"Now, what is it you want," I asked the animal, who calmed almost as soon as I arrived at his stall door. He towered over my small frame, but I did not feel threatened by him at all. "Why are you so excited?"

As my vision improved, I saw that I faced a tall blood bay horse, which appeared at first glance to be an Andalusian, though not the grey type I had seen in the stables over the years. His nostrils flared as he snorted at me and his dark eyes were nearly obscured by a massive forelock. I extended a hand to him, and watched him brace himself. It made me wonder if he had been struck by the liveryman recently. When I did not press him, the horse bent his neck down and extended his muzzle forward to sniff at my curled fingers, his warm moist breath tickling my palm. I am sure he could easily smell that I was not human, but this did not seem to frighten him in the least. It was almost as though I was being challenged by the fiery animal.

"Do not move, girl. He's a dangerous one," said the liveryman from somewhere behind me. I did not respond, but he continued to babble at me anyway. "He was sold to me cheaply because he very nearly killed his last rider. At the least, he has crippled him. He'll likely try the same with you."

The horse reared again, striking at the stall door with his hard black hooves. This time, I got a very good idea of his height, as even with his ears flattened to his skull, the very top his forelock brushed the low ceiling. It made Andreas' animal look like a child's pony in comparison. I spoke softly to the animal to try to calm him and in the same deceptively quiet tone, told the liveryman to step back. Far back. It took several minutes for the massive horse to calm down enough once more to approach me.

"Stand easy, sir," I told the horse softly, and uncurled my fingers to reveal a precious lump of rock sugar I had separated out from the bandits' loot. There were a few more secreted in the purse concealed in my blouse, but I left them there for now. The horse's velvet-soft lips rolled it around and across the palm of my hand a few times before he finally decided to take it into his mouth and eat it. Apparently having approved the offering, he began searching around for more, but there was none available, but he took another step forward and began sniffing up the length of my arm curiously. I stayed perfectly still, not wanting to destroy our precariously established peace. I could hear muted breathing behind me, as the liveryman tried very hard indeed to keep from breaking this fragile tableau, but I think he was worried more about his merchandise being damaged than my own well-being.

Asshole.

Moving very slowly, I unhooked the latch on the stall door and moved inside, closing it behind me. The horse shuddered in anticipation, but did not otherwise move, never taking his eyes from me. He had a massive chest, fine legs and well-shaped hooves. I could see some healing wounds on his chest that likely came from when he was dragged and otherwise manhandled into the tiny stall. I did not smell infection there, so they seemed to be doing well, despite the neglect they experienced at the moment.

I stretched out a hand to scratch his whiskery chin and moved upward on his lower jaw, still scratching, until I reached the broad space between his jawbones. The horse sighed deeply and then half-closed his eyes, his lips beginning to quiver on their own in response to the pleasant scratching. His coat was silky soft and his mane hung thick and low along his neck falling in both directions. I could not help twining the fingers of my other hand in it, feeling the delightful texture and finger combing the knots out of it in the process.

"Has he a name," I quietly asked the liveryman, who had not said a word in several minutes. The horse nickered softly and shoved his nose against my chest, lipping playfully at my blouse.

"The man who sold him to me never gave me one, miss," was the whispered reply. He seemed to have gathered up a bit more respect for me in the time since I had entered the stall. I looked the animal up and down, continuing to stroke his mane and leaning forward to smell the gloriously horsey scent that no other animal possesses. It was almost intoxicating.

"Ádhamh," I whispered into his ear, as he continued to nudge my midsection. "How do you like that for a name?"

He raised his nose level with my own and blew into my face, which I took as amiable equine laughter. He did not seem to mind my sense of humor, anyway. Moving carefully, I inspected the animal with my hands, finding that he was a stallion, rather than a gelding, in the process. His legs were well shaped, and his tendons seemed straight and not bowed, which was a blessing, and the upper arch of his neck was firm and in proportion to the rest of him, so he likely had never foundered. I felt no cracks in his hooves, which he allowed me to easily lift and inspect as well. I took the time to dig another piece of sugar out of my purse and handed it to him as a reward.

Satisfied with the horse's condition and not looking at what I was doing, I reached behind me and unlocked the stall door, after which I slowly backed out with Ádhamh following me. I heard the livery owner gasp in horror at my mendacity.

"You little fool! He'll run now and we'll never catch him again!" he whispered hoarsely from the stall into which I had thrown him. He was not stupid enough to come anywhere near either the horse or me. A point for him.

"I need a saddle and a bridle for him. I want nothing with a severe bit. I do not believe he needs that," I told the man. I could hear his muffled oath from where he hid. "I will give you fifteen pounds for him along with tack."

I heard his whispered profanity and waited for his response.

"Forty! He's a fine animal!" He countered.

"An animal who hates you and who will in all likelihood attempt to kill the next person who comes to consider him. Do you really want to *hang*?" I put all the derision and disgust I could into the last word, as I was tired of all this foolishness and had other things to do before I could resume my travels. He was muttering under his breath, but seemed to know I had him over the proverbial barrel. He really had no choice but to relent and accept my offer.

"Twenty pounds and not a shilling less. You can have the tack with which he arrived. It's not in the best shape, so its repair is up to you. I want the both of you gone, now!"

I removed the majority of the recently collected coins in my purse from their haven and tossed them into the straw. The liveryman could collect them when he had the time. I was through with him and his foolishness.

"Where is his tack, then? Give it to me and I will leave you forever," I spat, never taking my eyes from the horse, who seemed delighted by all the attention he was receiving.

The liveryman, not leaving his wooden fortress, gestured at a set of sawhorses near to where Ádhamh had been housed. I grabbed everything I saw there and walked out of the place, with my new horse following along behind me docilely. Once outside and in the sunlight, I put his gear on him. There were a few broken straps here and there, but there was nothing that could not be repaired on my next stop.

The townsfolk were abuzz with talk of the fire that had destroyed a row of shacks along the waterfront. I figuratively held my breath until I heard someone say in passing that "only Ged the taxman" had died in the conflagration. Indeed, no one seemed particularly upset at his passing, so I assumed that there would be no questions asked about the fire's origins. I was more than a little glad of that fact. Instead, they were more interested in discussing the way of his dying and seemed to feel that it reflected his enthusiasm in collecting taxes owed when he was younger. It seemed that no one would miss him.

Sad for him, but very good for me.

For form's sake, I took the reins loosely in my hand, but walked the short distance to the leather worker's shop, where he awaited me almost impatiently. When he saw Ádhamh, he stepped back. Apparently, he was familiar with the animal and wanted space between the great horse and him.

"Have you finished my order," I asked him. He wordlessly handed over a bundle of leather that had been carefully stitched and impressed with an attractive pattern. I nodded my satisfaction and then broached the next subject.

"I need you to repair the damaged tack on Ádhamh. Until it is fixed, I will not be able to mount him properly and go on my way." I tossed three shillings at the man and removed the saddle from the horse, leaving it with him. "I will return in two hours' time to recover the saddle. I expect you will have it finished by then."

He nodded dumbly, not even arguing over the price, and I turned away, leaping to Ádhamh's bare back and then riding away to the hills.

I thought it was time to allow the big horse to stretch out and exercise limbs that had been confined for who knew how long. Certainly long enough for the lash wounds to heal over halfway, anyway. It certainly explained why he had been so restive when I arrived that morning.

I had only ridden a few horses in my life thus far, and certainly nothing like the animal I now had the pleasure to actually own. He moved across the ground as I imagined flying might feel. He extended his legs as he ran, his neck bowed, tail held high in the air like a black silken banner. His mane whipped in my face, but that was okay, as he was enjoying himself. Every so often, he would let out a shrill scream, a challenge to any and all who might hear him. The feeling of his muscles as they worked, the sound of his hooves pounding into the dirt, was hypnotic, and I lost track of myself until I realized we were no longer moving and Ádhamh was standing in a small creek, for all the world as though he were cooling his hooves after the pounding he had given them.

I jumped down and let him drink a little bit of water, but pulled his head away from the stream after only a moment. He fought me a little bit, but his heart was not really in it. I already knew from speaking with the stable lads that letting a horse drink his fill after a long ride was asking for trouble, and I had no intention of losing my new mount to colic. I had seen it happen before, it was not pretty, and I had no need of or desire for horsemeat in my diet. He played in the water for a little bit, pawing at it and then slapping his hooves down, making the water splash. When he bored of that, he wandered over to the shore and began nibbling at the long blades of grass that lined it. Ádhamh startled a little when the bunch of grass he yanked out of the mud dislodged an unhappy frog that leapt away into the deeper part of the stream and swam madly away. A few soft words from me and he settled down, continuing to decimate the grassy bounty.

He suddenly alerted when a familiar sound came to my ears.

Mathúin had arrived and the two would finally meet. I knew that the dog would do as he was bid, but did not know what the horse's own experience with dogs might have been. I moved to stand between the two of them, wanting to divert any issues before they had the opportunity to rear their ugly heads. Mathúin's all-out run slowed to a trot and then a walk before he finally stopped at my side, his eyes on the massive horse who regarded him with a careful eye.

"Ádhamh, this is Mathúin. You are both mine and must learn to work together. I want no quarrelling between you," and then I moved away so they could meet one another unimpeded.

Dog and horse approached each other, stiff-legged, reaching out their respective muzzles to sniff at one another. The dog gave Ádhamh a quick lick on the end of his nose, which seemed to surprise the horse a bit. After a short time where he seemed to consider the dog who stood staring at him expectantly, Ádhamh rubbed his lips across the top of the big dog's head in a friendly manner, so I supposed that they would at least be tolerant of each other. Only time would tell, but so far, this was a good sign, as far as I was concerned.

I sat on the bank and watched them as they played after a fashion, with Ádhamh pretending to nip at Mathúin and the dog leaping backward at the last possible moment. A short chase game ensued, with the two taking turns as to who was "It". I could feel Mathúin's good humor in my head, so I knew there was no ill-feeling in him for the horse, and honestly, it was relaxing to watch them enjoy each other's company, so I let the play continue for a little while before I saw it was near noon and time to head back into town.

I returned to the leatherworker to pick up Ádhamh's repaired gear and saddled him up, laying the now-filled saddlebags I had ordered the day before behind it. The horse turned his head to nose at them curiously, and once satisfied, nudged at me with his muzzle, ready to go.

"Just a few more things left to do here, my friend, but the next one is all for you," I told him, scratching under his jaw and laughing with delight as I saw his lips begin to quiver in equine ecstasy. "You might not understand why it is something good for you, but it will keep you much safer as we travel."

I left the reins lying across his withers, and we all walked to the farrier, where I had the man re-shoe Ádhamh. I was concerned that one of the horse's shoes was getting loose, and it was best to get it all taken care of while I could. Throwing a shoe at an inconvenient time could very well cripple him, so it was better safe than sorry. Who knew when I would once more pass through a town with a farrier? I had seen what happened to horses to whom exactly that had occurred, and knew that they had faced a short future that would either end in a stewpot or dog kennel.

The farrier seemed a bit startled as we walked into his barn, apparently never having seen a horse walking freely beside its owner without actually being under its owner's direct control, but we were soon able to agree on a price for a complete re-shoeing. Mathúin, meanwhile, had settled down happily in a pile of the morning's hoof clippings and was now chewing on his stinking treasure. He had enjoyed such treats since the first day I met him, and it seemed had never outgrown his fascination and taste for a farrier's leavings.

After a few moments of concern from the farrier that the big animal might do him damage unless he was firmly and completely tied down, I assured him that Ádhamh was harmless. Thus, a short time later, I found myself standing at Ádhamh's head, scratching at his favorite place on his lower jaw as the farrier removed the old worn shoes and replaced them with new ones. To his credit, Ádhamh never moved a muscle during the entire process, allowing the farrier to pick up his feet, trim them to a turn and then apply the shoes.

Once we left the farrier, our last stop was the clothier, where I purchased some long linen blouses in off-white and dark brown, two pair of dark trousers and a yard or so of plain soft cloth. I did not want anything fancy or out of the ordinary, but was still careful to purchase men's clothing, rather than a woman's wardrobe. Anyhow, women's clothing was designed for riding sidesaddle, not astride, so that was yet another reason it certainly would not do to purchase it.

The tailor did not even attempt to argue with me, he seemed happy just to get my custom. Perhaps sales were slow right now with the religious unrest between the English interlopers and us Irish. Whatever the reason, I was just glad that I encountered no argument there.

A trip to the cobbler's shop immediately thereafter secured a used though still serviceable leather belt, a wide-brimmed dark leather hat and a pair of soft leather boots that went to my knees. The cobbler gave me an odd look, as I was purchasing decidedly male attire.

"And why is a lass like yourself buying a man's clothing? Proper young ladies do not dress in such a fashion," he confronted me as I stood at his desk to make my purchase. "I have clothing appropriate for a young lady on the other side of my shop. Certainly you saw it when you came in!"

"I am traveling a long distance on horseback, so this is what I need. I have the coin to pay for it, so do not trouble yourself over my choice of clothing," I replied, putting money atop his desk and turning to walk out, my purchases in my hand.

"Fine, lass, if you insist on buying these items, at least allow me to package them for you," and he limped out from behind his desk and took the clothing from me as he also took up a largish piece of frayed woolen cloth and a piece of string. I was too shocked at his audacity to protest and simply allowed him to continue doing as he liked. I thought my business here was finished, but then a large dark brown leather satchel caught my eye. It was hanging on a hook, nearly concealed by a worn woolen cloak, and I could not resist asking about it.

"Uhm, that satchel over there, sir; is it for sale?" The man turned to look where I was pointing and his eyes widened in recognition.

"Well, it had been intended for another customer, but he is two weeks late in coming to claim it, so I suppose you can have it, if you like.

In fact, take it with my blessing! Good luck to you on your journey, wherever it may be taking you."

When he was done, I thanked him warmly for his kindness and unexpected generosity and left, making straight for Ádhamh and Mathúin, who waited for me outside. I had stayed in town a little too long for my comfort and it was time to go.

Chapter Ten

When I left the shop, Ádhamh nickered a welcome and Mathúin wagged his tail, happily welcoming me back. The dog nosed at the package in my hand, as though he hoped it contained treats for him, but I had to disappoint him.

"Sorry, laddie, but this is all for me. I do not think you would look particularly attractive wrapped in clothing." He snorted at me and then started down the center of the street, apparently more than ready to leave town. Perhaps he was picking up on my own desire to be on my way as well. He stopped when he was a few yards away, looking over his shoulder in his impatience to be away.

I placed the package into one of the saddlebags where my new clothing already rested and put my new hat on my head, securing it beneath my chin with a lanyard. I immediately was pleased with my hat, as it shaded my eyes and face from the brightness of the sun.

Then I swung up onto Ádhamh's back and rode out of town at an easy pace, as I did not want to gather any more attention than was strictly necessary. Once we were out of sight of town, however, I put my heels to his flanks and we shot forward, covering more than a few miles in a matter of an hour's hard ride. I gave the horse his head and let him run until he slowed on his own. Mathúin ran hard to keep up with us, and though he was breathing hard when we finally slowed enough for him to stay abreast of us, he still seemed happy.

Knowing that coming to a stop at this point would be bad for Ádhamh's health, I kept him at a walk for a few miles while his muscles unknotted and his breathing eased to a regular and unlabored rhythm. He shook his head up and down, trying to get the bit between his teeth, but I was careful to keep control of it through my hold on the reins. I knew he had enjoyed the run immensely, but I also had to remember that I was his mistress and that he had to listen to me. Giving him his head would never be something that happened on a regular basis.

It was mid-afternoon when we came across a pond and stopped so both Ádhamh and Mathúin could drink. I took the time to unsaddle the horse and once he had drunk his fill, rubbed him down with the blouse that I had been wearing until that time, once I had wet it down.

I had to rinse the blouse several times while I wiped the caked salt from his coat and wiped the gunk out of his eyes. I spent extra time rubbing his legs, massaging them to help release any knots therein. He seemed to enjoy the extra attention and nibbled idly at the crown of my head as I worked.

Once I had gotten him as clean as I could, short of standing him under a convenient waterfall, I rinsed out the blouse, now little better than a rag, and bathed myself as well. It felt wonderful to be able to finally bathe and not be cleaning massive amounts of filth and blood from my skin. I carefully washed the rude bandage I had put over my chest wound and draped it over a rock to dry. I was glad that it did not seem to leak much, but knew I would have to address it sooner, rather than later as it was more than a small nuisance.

Ádhamh seemed a bit surprised to see my naked flesh, but then, he had likely never seen a naked female human, much less a naked female vampire. In my experience, horses are like cats, and are terribly curious creatures at heart. I laughed as he suddenly ducked his head, kicked his rear legs in the air and dashed into the woods. There was something in me that knew he would not go far. Mathúin ran after him. I could feel in my head that he was far more concerned about the horse's whereabouts than I.

When I was satisfied that I was clean, I left the pond and dried myself thoroughly. My unnaturally pale skin was uncomfortable in direct sunlight, so I moved to the shade of an obliging tree to complete the process. I had rarely been unclothed in direct sunlight since my death, so I had not realized how uncomfortable its unabated rays could make me. The sunlight did not actually burn me, but did feel unnaturally hot against my skin.

I put a clean wad of cotton over the still very small open wound in my chest, then bound my breasts and with them, the wound, with several yards of cotton cloth. It was easiest to be seen as male when my breasts were not quite so visible to the casual watcher. The loose blouses would aid in the careful deception as well.

Ádhamh returned as I was dressing and grazed a bit while he had the opportunity. The lush grass was almost irresistible to the horse, and certainly much better than the fare he had been given in the stable. He finished a mouthful of grass and nickered approval into my face as he inspected the now clean and properly clothed me. He sniffed at my bound breasts as though wondering what had happened to the naked bits with which he had earlier seen me.

Mathúin emerged from the trees with the fresh carcass of a rabbit in his jaws and lay down to eat it while he waited for me. I chose not to watch and was glad that I could not smell it unless I deliberately inhaled through my nose. The whole process of watching someone or something consume solid food made me feel a bit ill now. Instead, I made a big business of once again finger combing the tangles from Ádhamh's long and full mane and then his tail, which he tolerated with grace, and then I carefully braided his mane to keep it from tangling further.

I really needed to pick up a decent comb somewhere to make this an easier process.

In a few minutes, Mathúin had wolfed down the remains of the rabbit and I had done what I could with the horse's generous natural adornments and so it was time to ride on. I leapt into the saddle and away we went, with me being careful to keep Ádhamh at no more than an easy canter, the day being beautiful and calm, and with me in no particular hurry to get anywhere.

We had gone some five miles before I heard something up ahead. The sounds of raucous laughter and jeering assaulted my ears and I pulled Ádhamh up short, not wanting to ride into whatever was going on up the road. I smelled blood and fear in the air, and determined that they had a captive of some sort with them. Swinging down from the big horse, I took him to the side of the road and bade him stay there, looping his reins around a convenient tree branch to keep him where I had left him.

"It is better that you stay here and out of harm's way. I will be back to get you when things are safe," I told him, not sure whether he understood me or not.

He nickered unhappily, but stayed. Mathúin, on the other hand, seemed eager to participate in whatever lay ahead.

I kept to the side of the road, using the trees to conceal myself as I approached the situation. The smell of fear grew stronger and my fangs slipped down of their own accord. The scent excited me tremendously, and I realized that I would need to learn to exert more control over myself if I were to blend in with humanity in the cities. I knew that if I had hackles, they would be raised, as indeed were Mathúin's. The rough gray hair along his spine was lifted, giving him a bristly appearance which, when combined with his mouthful of fangs, made him a not insignificant consideration.

When I reached the source of the disturbance, I found a man who was all trussed up and at the mercy of a pair of men dressed in good leather tunics and pants. One held a knife to the bound man's throat and laughed. It was a merciless laugh full of ugliness and contempt.

"I do not think you have a choice, swordsmith. You will come with us and do as our lord demands. If you are lucky and do a decent job, he just might allow you to live," that unworthy said, an ugly look on his face, in heavily accented Gaelic. I suspected he and his companion were Englishmen and my dislike increased. The man opened another of what seemed a dozen tiny holes on his captive's cheek with the point of his dagger.

Their captive writhed in his bonds, screaming for mercy, his eyes wild.

"I cannot do this for him, sir! The sword is broken and cannot be remade," he gasped out. His torturer was having none of it.

"Then I suppose you'll just have to die then, fool!" and the man drew back his dagger to plunge it into his victim's throat. "You had your chance."

His knife never met its target, as I leaped forward and grabbed his arm, spoiling his aim and causing its point to go wide. Mathúin engaged the second man, keeping him occupied while I addressed the first, who responded to my interference by screaming some English oath. He spun around and jerked his arm out of my hand, now waving his dagger in my face. His scream as he saw my fangs brought him up short and suddenly *he* was the one in terror. He glanced over at his friend and was met with the sight of Mathúin tearing out the man's throat, leaving him gurgling on the ground, his lifeblood pouring out into the dirt.

"What seems to be the problem here? I believe this man has told you 'no' about something you want him to do," I said to him in English. "Perhaps 'no' is the answer you should accept and go on your way. Of course, you could always choose the destination your friend there apparently decided upon."

"This was none of your business, bitch!" he snarled at me. "If you had passed on, I might have let you live."

It was almost pathetic to see such bravado from a sadly doomed man. Rather than interfere in our little tableau, Mathúin moved to sit next to the bound man, but never took his eyes from what I was doing.

"You have made it my business. The word 'no' cannot be misconstrued to mean 'yes'. Leave now and *I* might let *you* live," told him curtly.

Instead of replying, the man came at me, swinging his dagger at my face.

Why is it that so many men choose violence to respond, rather than using their words? I really do not know. I had not done him any real harm yet, so why was his immediate response to try to harm *me*? At least my agility and speed gave me the advantage I needed in this fight.

I jerked backward and narrowly avoided getting a mouthful of the blade, but his strong downstroke cut into my blouse and over my breastbone, cutting deeply into the flesh there. I hissed with pain and uttered a profane oath as I angrily kicked out with one of my feet, sweeping his legs out from under him and knocking him to the ground in the process. That accomplished, I leapt atop him, pinning his arms in the dirt and bringing my face down close to his so he would not miss my next words.

"I do not care what lord may have sent you on this fool's errand, but it ends now. You English seem to think you may run roughshod over us Irish and get away with it. Well, in this case, I will not allow that to happen."

He squirmed beneath me, trying to bring his knife hand up, but I knocked that hand down against the ground hard and the knife flew from his hand to land in the grass a few feet away. I watched as his eyes followed the knife's trajectory and the anguish that covered him as it landed further away than he could easily reach and he realized he was done for.

"Please! Please! Let me go! Don't kill me," he whimpered, crocodile tears running down his temples as he pleaded for his worthless life. His gaze seemed locked on my chest wound, and no longer on my fangs. Apparently, this was not sorting out the way he might have liked.

Too bad.

I looked up and over at the bound man whose predicament had brought us all to this tableau. His eyes were still wide, but his struggling had ceased. I could see his eyes were fixed on the ragged tear in my blouse and the small amount of blood that stained the frayed ends of the violated cloth. I could almost read his mind as he tried to understand why there was not more blood flowing down the front of my chest. He would soon get a rude awakening.

Trails of now drying blood had trickled down his face from the countless knife pricks this ass has bestowed upon him, and it seemed to me as though he would not be able to escape scarring. It saddened me a bit, as he was not an unattractive fellow, and it would be a crime if women avoided him, thinking he had contracted and then recovered from the pox. His unusually green eyes met mine and for a moment, we shared a moment of perfect clarity and I knew what my next move would be.

"I believe the answer is 'no,'" I told the man beneath me, returning my full attention to him. "Perhaps you should have listened the first time you heard it said."

A wail of despair cut the air like one of the *bean sí* foretelling someone's passing.

With that, I opened a large hole in his throat and left him to bleed to death on the ground as I got up and dusted the dust from my knees. I did not drink his blood, as the bound man seemed traumatized enough by what he had just witnessed. I will admit that it was nice not have to worry about washing up again, either. I rose from the ground and walked over to the bound man, my fangs once again concealed within my gums. It seemed that once the excitement was over with, they went away on their own.

That was a happy discovery, to say the least.

Chapter Eleven

"Do not be afraid. I will not harm you," I told the man as I went over and began to untie him. His hands were just starting to turn blue from inhibited blood flow, so I was just in time to keep him from serious bodily damage. If he were indeed a swordsmith, it would not do for him to lose his livelihood. I took a moment and rubbed my hands over his to encourage the flow of blood to his fingers and then walked a little bit away to sit enough of a distance away that he would not necessarily panic over what he had seen.

"Thank you for saving me," he breathed. His voice was now very quiet. Perhaps he was afraid that I would be startled if he had spoken in a normal tone of voice. "I don't know what I can do to possibly repay you for your timely arrival. "

I could see the question in his bright green eyes and nodded at him, once. It did not take him long.

"What are you?"

There was no way he had not seen my fangs, so this question really did not surprise me. I considered for a few minutes before I responded. In for a penny, in for a pound, as they say.

"I am a vampire," I told him. "At least, that is what my maker told me when I asked him what I was now. I will not harm you. We Irish should stick together."

He gave me a wan smile and even managed a chuckle, which surprised me a bit. He crouched on the ground and reached out a careful hand to Mathúin who was in the process of sniffing him up and down. When the big dog did not growl or try to bite, the man rubbed his back, and I chuckled as Mathúin surrendered to the attention. Since my four-legged guardian trusted him, I could do no less.

"What is a *vampire*," he asked, stumbling a bit over the strange word. "Is this *vampire* thing what keeps you from bleeding?"

He gestured at my chest, causing me to look down at the new tear in my flesh and I started a bit when I saw that the wound exposed the bit of metal that was lodged in there. Involuntarily, I found my hand rising to try to dig it out. It was painful to poke at it, and I blistered the air with an oath that made my new friend wince as if he was the one in pain.

"Apologies to you for my unladylike profanity, but I was in pain and could not control it. I was wounded a few days ago and it will not heal completely while the piece of metal you can see here is still lodged in my rib," I told him. "This seemed as good a time as any to try to remove it."

I dug at it a bit more and only succeeded in digging long trenches in my talons. It was clear that I was getting nowhere, fast.

So I was surprised when the man suddenly moved forward and grabbed up the knife from the ground where it had fallen. He seemed rather accustomed to holding such things and I now found myself wondering just who I had now rescued. Would I now find myself battling the man I had killed two others to save?

But he surprised me even further with his next words.

"I will not hurt you, miss, but I can help you get that thing out," he told me, his eyes earnest and surprisingly calm and kind. "It is but the work of a moment."

Who was I to turn down such an offer of assistance? Nodding acquiescence, I allowed him to approach me and he hunkered down in front of me, asking silent permission to touch my bare skin.

This *was* 1600's Ireland, after all. Random touching was something that was just not *done* at that place and time unless you were married to the woman you touched, or she was a whore who just did not care what you did to her as long as she was well recompensed for the liberties you took with her.

I nodded my permission and he put the knife to the wounded rib. Digging gingerly, he worked at the piece of metal for a moment or two and then suddenly it came free and he popped it into my hand. It was longer than I had thought it was, coming out at being half again as large as I had estimated.

"Thank you! I don't know how I would have accomplished that on my own. It is difficult to work on yourself at that angle."

"You will need to bind that wound so that it will heal now, miss," he told me. I shook my head dismissively.

"No, it is not as easy as that. I need to feed in order to heal. Only then will it all close up again," I told him wryly. "I will have to wait until I may feed again."

"Feed?" He seemed to catch the idea that the word *feed* had nothing to do with conventional victuals.

"I do not consume food as you do anymore. I am only able to feed upon fresh human blood."

He moved backward so quickly that he *plopped* down onto his buttocks hard enough to make the dust rise around his breeches. He very suddenly appeared to be quite scared of me once more.

"You are safe from me, sir. You are not on my menu," I assured him with what I hoped was a warm smile. As I no longer thought like a human, I had to try to remember how to do certain things. Vampires think and respond very differently than a human being does, but it appeared that this time I got it right. "I will find my sustenance elsewhere from a more appropriate source."

"Are you not able to *feed* upon one of these two persons," he asked me, putting a stress on the verb. I shook my head in the negative.

"I have already discovered that I am unable to do just that. I need to wait until I may feed upon someone whose heart still beats within his breast. The dead blood from these two is poison to my body."

I saw him turn at bit green at this revelation, but points to him for not running away, screaming in terror. My estimation of his innate good sense rose enormously.

"How did all of this happen to you? Was it a curse?" he asked me carefully.

"I am not certain, myself. I was as human as you until a short time ago. I was attacked by another such as myself and woke up as you see me now." I saw his gaze shift to the man I had killed and I hastened to add, "It is not as simple as my killing someone to make them come back a vampire, as I have learned."

"That is probably a good thing," he replied after a moment's thought and even managed a small chuckle, with which I could not help but join in.

"What is your name? I am called Siofra."

I felt fairly stupid for not having asked his name earlier, especially as we were now so intimately acquainted. He seemed not to have noticed the lapse in decorum, for which fact I was more than a little grateful. A vampire I might be, but manners are still necessary when one is not currently embroiled in the process of defending their very existence. I probably should not have given him the name by which I was called, but he did not make me feel threatened in the least.

"I must say that I am more than a little pleased to have made your timely acquaintance, Mistress Siofra. The gods, themselves must have had a hand in your arrival in my hour of need. I am called Simon," he told me. "Simon the sword maker, from Dublin. I'm not the best at my craft, but people do speak well of my work. I was captured by these Englishmen to reforge a blade belonging to their master. I do not reforge blades made by others, as I will not be responsible if something happens to it. As you can see, they refused to understand that." He gingerly felt the damage that had been done to his face and grimaced.

Ah, he was an artisan, and one who was proud of his own work and reputation. I could understand that completely, as I had known a few like him in my life. I nodded to let him know that I agreed with him.

"I do understand you, Simon the sword maker," I told him. "Will this lord know where you live and come after you when his men do not return?"

"The men were sent out to collect *a* sword maker, not me in particular. I really do not know what may happen if he thinks to inquire," he replied. He smiled a bit ruefully. "I suppose this only comes of being good at what I do. I gather that they asked around before settling on me and assume they were directed to me by someone in town. At first they entreated me to come with them voluntarily, but when I refused, they treated me as you saw. Part of me suspected that were I to accompany them that I would have had a very difficult time returning to my home in Dublin."

This last was something that was not unheard of, being very like the press gangs that would randomly go out into a village and kidnap people into Navy service. Once you were in, it was very difficult to get back out again. Some lords would "press" talented individuals into their own households in much the same way. That two men had been sent to collect him in the first place implied that this had been the plan all along.

"Why were you stopped on the road? I would think they would have taken you to your intended destination before continuing their games?"

"The one *you* killed, Dobb, liked to hurt people, and I think he was bored from all that riding from Dublin. So he stopped to entertain himself a bit." He started a bit when Ádhamh began making noise from around the bend. Holding up my index finger to Simon for a moment's time, I jumped up and ran to where the horse was tied, releasing him before he broke his reins, then came back to Simon and sat down again to continue our conversation. I did not bother leading him over to where I was, as I was certain he would follow me on his own.

The man's eyes about popped out of his head when Ádhamh came around the corner a moment later, his head and tail raised proudly and looking glorious. The big horse wandered over to me and stood above me, his bristly lips playing with my hair. When I squeaked feigned indignation, he changed his target and began nuzzling at my purse, looking for treats. To reward him for his good behavior, I dug one of my precious lumps of sugar out of my purse and gave it to him. Simon simply stared at what went on before his eyes. One might think he had never before seen a friendly horse. I took the opportunity to dig in one of my bags for a fresh blouse and length of clean gauze to cover my new and larger wound.

"That is your animal?" he asked me, never taking his eyes from Ádhamh. I nodded as I dressed my wound and then donned the new blouse. When I was done, I spent a little extra time with Ádhamh and scratched companionably beneath the horse's extensive forelock. "I believe I know this horse, but it cannot be the same animal!"

"Why is that?" I responded.

"The horse I am thinking of is a vicious brute that nearly killed Lord Bramby's valet, but this animal is gentle as a lamb!" he cried. I smiled knowingly.

"I am quite certain that this is the same animal. I only just purchased him from the livery a few miles from here. He was intent on killing the fool of an owner, but I helped him think better of it." I laid a hand under the horse's lips and waited as I allowed him to explore the palm of my hand with his soft mouth. Every so often one or more of his whiskers would tickle my skin and my hand would twitch in response.

"That horse was supposed to be destroyed and a man was paid to get rid of it. It seems he decided to make his money off a living animal. You are lucky you are still..." his words trailed off as he realized that he was not speaking to a living, breathing woman, and he clapped a hand to his lips as though that would make those unwise words disappear. Perhaps he still feared for his life. There was something sad about the fact that even now, after I had saved his life and released him from his bonds, there remained some small part of him that feared me. This did not bode well at all for future relationships.

"Yes, you are correct. I am no longer amongst the living, but as I told you earlier, you have nothing to fear from me. I wish you would believe me when I say that," I told him. He had the grace to look embarrassed.

"I am very sorry, Miss. You appeared like one of the *Leannán sí*, seemingly out of nowhere, and then between that great hound and yourself, you kill both my tormentors. I feel as though I owe a life debt to the *sí* for this." He was babbling, but what I established was that he thought I was one of the faerie folk and that I had saved his life in order to create a debt between us. "Please tell me what I must do to dissolve this debt you hold over my head."

It appeared that I would be unable to dissuade him from thinking I was one of the Faerie folk, so instead I played along. There was indeed something I needed, and he seemed to be the man who could make that happen for me.

"You call yourself a sword maker. Then I charge you to make for me a matched pair of boot knives, double edged and of good strong steel. Sharp enough to shave with, if need be. Can you do that for me?" He appeared to consider my request.

"It will take a few days, but yes, I can do that, if you are able to wait that long," he told me with calm self-assurance. "I would need you nearby to take your measurements and be sure they are properly balanced…if that is not an issue for you, of course."

I thought about what he said, and decided that a decent set of knives would not be something unreasonable for which to wait, and that the knives would be made to my measurements, made them doubly valuable to me. I had kept the broken knife I had taken from the bandits, but it was designed for a larger hand than my own, and with a broken tip, it would be more difficult to wield, should I need a sharp knife tip to accomplish a task.

"Yes, I can make the time, Master Simon," I told him as I brushed the dust from my trousers and stretched as best I could without pulling the edges of my wound far enough to cause too much pain. "I thank you for your kind consideration."

Having come to an agreement, I spent a few minutes catching up one of the better of the three horses that had belonged to the now dead thugs and bid Simon ride upon it. As comfortable as I might feel around him, I had no desire to have him at my back for a ride all the way back to Dublin.

Simon was an accomplished conversationalist, which I found somewhat surprising, having known a few blacksmiths in my life and found them to be rather curt in their verbal exchanges. Perhaps Dublin was a more friendly and patient town than the very small and particularly insular communities in which I had been raised.

During our time together on the road, I learned about his lady love, a young woman called Cecily, who was near to bearing their second child. His first was a son called Peregrine. When I asked about the unusual name, he laughed and told me that his own father was called Peregrine, so he felt honor bound to bestow the rather ostentatious family name on the tyke.

Simon seemed concerned about my chest wound, but I assured him that all would be well with me and not to fret about it. Indeed I felt a certain amount of hunger, but would not feed on the affable man and knew that I would likely find a suitable meal somewhere within the confines of Dublin, which was a well-traveled enough city that all manner of souls, pure and otherwise, passed through it on a daily basis. I need only control myself long enough to do so.

When we finally reached Dublin, the aroma of so much concentrated humanity nearly drove me to distraction, as hungry as I had become over our journey. I could feel my fangs attempting to push their way to the fore, and I had to hold my mouth very still to keep them from showing and frightening the folk who looked at us as we entered the town. Some hailed Simon as we passed obviously pleased that he had returned relatively unscathed.

They gave me odd looks, as now I was not even bothering to try to hide my feminine appearance, and it was more than a little unusual to see any woman, much less one as tiny as I, mounted astride what could only be a war horse. Mathúin, displaying a showmanship I had not known he possessed, trotted alongside us, ignoring all in our path.

Simon's home and shop were on the far side of Dublin, near the water. I suppose it made sense to have one's forge near to where ingots and ore were unloaded from trade vessels. Why should one have to haul their supplies any further than was absolutely necessary? He said as much to me when I finally asked him why he would want to live so close to the stink of the docks.

His wife, Cecily, wrapped me in a sisterly embrace when Simon introduced me as the author of his escape and heroic return, crying on my shoulder as she thanked me over and over for my intercession and subsequent rescue of her beloved husband. It did not seem to occur to her that it was wildly unlikely that someone such as me would be able to affect such a feat against two burly men armed with deadly weapons, but I chose not to bring that fact to her attention.

His son, Peregrine, a tow headed boy of about four, entangled himself about my legs and chanted my name over and over in his high child's voice. He seemed to like the sound of it, though with some encouragement from his parents, shortly changed his chant to "Auntie Siofra".

It was difficult not to visibly cringe at his enthusiasm, but then, children had never been my favorite creatures upon this earth. Some folk are well suited to being with youngsters, but that has ever been my failing. In this case, however, I kept my opinions to myself and fancied that I accepted Peregrine's enthusiastic attention gracefully.

At least, I hoped it was graceful. I could be wrong.

That night, while Simon, Cecily and young Peregrine slept, I sated my hunger on a scurvy-tainted sailor who had drunk entirely too much and now slept against a barrel on the dock, too wobbly to make his way to his hammock below decks. While he did not taste particularly wonderful, his blood did its job and repaired the damage I had taken in the fight which freed Simon. When I was done, I threw the man's body into the water, knowing that I should be safe from discovery. Sailors rarely came to a good end, and this one would be just another one who died badly.

After I was done feeding, Mathúin and I slept the rest of the night away in an abandoned building at the end of the docks, taking care to bolt the door to keep out unwanted company. The rats that infested the building made a good meal for the hungry dog, once he was able to catch them.

You may ask why I did not rest with the smith's family that night, which is a reasonable question, and I will tell you why I did not:

Although I considered the human family to be friends of a sort, I was not comfortable enough to give them the chance to expose me to the community at large. While gratitude at my actions may have made them happily disposed toward me, who is to say that a desire for further fame on their part might not ultimately inspire them to reveal me and my kind to the world?

Chapter Twelve

I think I remember so much about my encounter with Simon the blacksmith so long ago because, believe it or not, I still have one of the two blades he forged for me over a week's time. They helped me to defend myself when it was necessary that I conceal my true self quite literally hundreds of times.

The one that was lost was taken in a terrible battle that nearly cost me my life. So, while I might mourn a bit over its loss, I am, nevertheless, grateful that the circumstances of its loss allowed me to survive.

The blades were forged beautifully, and Simon took the time to be sure that they were perfectly balanced in my small hands. The wooden hilt was of a black stained wood that he polished to a high luster, and was then decorated with an intricate pattern of Celtic knots. I believe that he did this because part of him still believed me to be one of the *Leannán sí,* and he wanted to make and keep me happy with him and his work.

The day he presented me with the finished blades, I embraced him gladly and thanked him effusively for the fine work he had done in creating them. Against his will, I pressed a few coins on him in appreciation of what he had made for me. When he protested further regarding payment, I bade him keep the coins against a dowry for his next child, should it be a daughter. Grudgingly, he acceded to my request and handed the coins off to Cecily, who clutched them to her breast as though they were a lifeline.

When we parted, I possessed a fine pair of double-edged boot knives sharp enough to shave a heavy beard and a new pair of custom-made soft and supple boots onto which a pair of sturdy sheaths had been installed to contain the aforementioned knives. The tops of the boots went to just below my knees, giving the blades plenty of room to lie along the outside of my calves and making it less likely that either the points or sharp edges would damage the leather any more than was absolutely necessary.

For a time, while I learned more about myself, we three traveled over the length and breadth of Ireland. I had decided that I needed to know my abilities and limitations as thoroughly as I was able to manage before I left the country and set sail for the Continent. It made sense to me that doing so in an area where I would not stand out quite so much was probably the best way to do that.

It seems as though I required more frequent feeding in my first several months as a vampire. While the majority of my transformation had been accomplished in the three days it took me to first rise as a Child of Blood, other things required more time to complete. Although I did not know it at the time, most of my inert human organs save for my lungs were slowly being replaced with nearly the same kind of spongy flesh that my formerly human flesh had become, my empty and useless intestines being amongst the first to undergo this bizarre transmogrification.

For a time, I merely wandered from place to place, camping in grassy and rodent infested ruins where I would leave both horse and dog to feed themselves as I slept. Generally, I only slept in inhabited areas when I absolutely could not avoid it, as I did not feel I had learned to control my appetite well enough to trust myself completely. During that time, my food most often consisted of bandits or lone English soldiers who ventured too far away from the safety of numbers. I will admit that it was more than a little satisfying to dine upon the English invaders. They had invaded our country and stolen the food from our fields and the mouths of Irish children. I felt it was more than appropriate that I fed upon them.

I was not always so heartless. There were times when I stayed my seemingly bottomless hunger. Sometimes, when it was not someone I would already be predisposed to see dead and I had the option, I would drink a small amount of blood, providing I found them already unconscious and could leave them alive, rather than killing them. This generally required making a more cunningly created wound with one of my very fine knives from which to feed and then being thoughtful enough to clean and bind the wound after I finished.

During my several months on my own, I discovered that while my hair does not grow, it would return to the length it was before cutting, should I choose to feed. When I cut off my hair, the bits that are cut off instantly turn white and become dull, dry and wispy, as though it was hair from an older person. I learned that bit of information one day when I chose to cut my hair to better pass as a male. When I need to appear to be male, I cut my hair to shoulder length and tie it into a tidy queue at the nape of my neck. As long as I do not feed while my hair is cut short, it will stay at the length I have chosen, but once I feed, it grows as though it is participating in a foot race.

It seems that losing mass is not in the cards for me unless I fail to feed. This is also true in the event that I inconveniently lose a digit or limb. Trust me when I tell you that both losing the body part and what comes next can be disgusting to behold. The severed limb simply disintegrates into a loose pile of dust as soon as it parts from my body, including the bone. It is impossible to tell that it was ever a limb.

Restoring an entire limb requires that I drink a significant amount of blood which my body then uses to repair itself. As I said before, the regrowth process is positively grotesque. First, bone and cartilage emerge from the area to where the limb would be attached. Then internal flesh and nerves crawl out over the bone. Thereafter, fibers that apparently simulate veining for the limb in question overlay the spongy flesh, and then finally, skin grows out from the existing skin to cover it all again, including any of the scars I collected before I became a vampire. Sadly, this tends to be a slower process than that of my hair growing back. After a time or two watching in horrified fascination, I avoided watching it happen at any opportunity. While the whole thing makes me feel incredibly nauseous, you may recall that the way my internal organs are designed, I am unable to vomit, much as I might like to do so.

If I am otherwise "healthy", feeding usually means having at least a pint of blood every two or three days, providing I am not repairing significant damage. A few times, I have had only partial regeneration until I could feed again to finish the process, and yes, that time in between was painful, considering that I would have exposed and very raw nerve endings unprotected by a covering of skin.

I have never intentionally created another vampire. There was one time when I created one by accident, causing me to discover how I had been made, but I destroyed that one as quickly as I discovered what I had inadvertently done. It had happened in a place and time when it would have been terrible to attempt to raise a fledgling vampire, so I really had no choice in the matter.

Being a vampire has its benefits and its shortcomings, there is no doubt about that in my mind. To the casual person, the idea of living forever might seem so very romantic, but it can be mind-numbing and cause unutterable despair in those who experience it. Yes, some vampires do end up destroying themselves with fire or even beheading when it gets to be too much for them and they cannot bear to exist another day, but as yet, I had not reached that point.

Perhaps someday in the future that might occur, but for now, it's not in the cards. I am too self-confident and maybe a bit too self-absorbed to take that final leap.

Epilogue

...D^{ub.} I stared down at him, shocked to hear that his heart still beat. There was something in this man that kept him from completely letting go, but I knew that his determination could not last forever. It was as though I could feel him all around me, begging me to do what only I could do for him. A silent whisper rode the wind, egging me on as I gazed dumbly down at him.

Seemingly of its own accord, my right hand reached down and pulled my single remaining dagger from its sheath. In one fluid movement, it sliced into my left forearm, causing a small amount of blood to pool there. Pulling the man's mouth open, I shoved my arm up against his tongue, squeezing what little blood I could out of my own flesh and making a small puddle of the stuff on his tongue. I instantly closed his mouth and raised him up enough that his head was tilted back and my blood, formerly his own blood, was able to flow down his throat and down into his body again.

It does not take much blood at all to trigger the transformation. That was how it had happened to me, all those centuries ago, when I had tried to fight free by biting my own maker. If I had but surrendered to my fate, I would have died along with everyone else in the castle.

Right now, I found that I could smell the changes already beginning to spark within his body. It is a smell unlike anything a mortal human being has even discovered. It did not matter if his body died now that the change had begun, as I had started the process before his heart ceased to beat.

I gathered up my fledgling and stood, holding him close to my chest. I was now his mother in fact, and would need to raise him and teach him the right and wrong of being a vampire in the modern age. I heard his heart make its final thump and felt his body relax as he died, but knew from my own experience that his mind was trapped inside his body, trying to make sense of the confusing signals around it. Until he woke as a Child of Blood, I would not be able to explain what had happened to him.

He might curse me for what I had done to him, and if that was the case, I would offer to end his suffering, but something told me it was time for me to bring another of my kind into the world. Odd to have something like a maternal instinct pop up four hundred years into my existence, but that is what happened here.

I raced to my current lodgings in a loft apartment in the city, bypassing the front entrance with its nighttime rent-a-cop to slide in the back entryway and get upstairs to my own unit without showing up in the ever-present security cameras. Once I got the man inside, I stripped him down and brought him into the shower with me to wash him off, as he had soiled himself when his body died. He had what appeared to be an appendectomy scar, but was otherwise unblemished.

He was a little over six feet in height, and solidly built, with a well-developed set of abdominal muscles. Nothing you might call "six-pack abs", but neither was it anything to sneeze at. His skin was already pale, though not quite as pale as my own. His thick, slightly wavy hair was a soft brown color, and was cut to just below the back of his skull, leaving his longish neck quite bare. He was also fortunate enough that his "five o'clock shadow" was so short as to be almost non-existent, so he would not need to go through eternity looking like a refugee from a 1970's television series.

Once I had gotten him cleaned up, I dried him carefully and then placed him on my couch. It was an awful vinyl thing, but that was fine, since he might still lose things that his body no longer needed over the following three days it would take for him to awaken. I placed a towel strategically over his man bits, so that I did not have to look at them, and then I went to my own rest in the small bedroom that adjoined the living room.

I did not leave the apartment for the entire three days, which my hunger did not appreciate at all, but I felt it would be wrong for me to leave this man to his own devices. I slept most of the time I waited, as it was the best way to avoid acting on my hunger. He had had no identification on him when I discovered him, so I had taken to calling him "child" when I addressed his slumbering form.

"Rest, child. It is only a matter of time before we can finally introduce ourselves. Do not be afraid," was a frequent litany from me as I stroked his cold forehead and petted him as he changed.

On the evening of the third day, I heard noises from the living room and left my reading of internet news sites at the computer in my bedroom to see what was happening. I found my fledgling sitting up on the couch, staring at his changed arms and hand, which had taken on that same unnatural perfection mine had some four hundred years previous to today. I know he heard me enter the room, because I suddenly found myself staring into a pair of the most beautiful blue-gray eyes I had ever seen. There was a terror in his slightly unfocused eyes that tore at my heart.

"Who are you? What's happened to me?"

"Easy now, child. You are not what you once were," I told him, moving carefully to sit beside him on the couch. I saw his nose working and knew that he could smell me. I found that I was able to scent that this was my own child, as there was something of me to his aroma. Perhaps it had to do with the fact that he was created from the blood I had ingested, even though it had once been his own. "I'm here to answer your questions, if I am able."

"What...what am I? And what are you?"

"You and I are vampires, child. I found you dying in an alley and against my better judgment, created you as a Child of Blood. I have never done this in my nearly four hundred years as a *sumaire*. You are my first. I am Siofra Bodhrán. What is your name, child?"

He stared at me for a long time as he digested this startling and alien information I supplied. I knew he was hungry and that we would both have to find somewhere we could both feed. I had some ideas on that, but for now, I needed to gauge his reactions to see whether or not he would survive to see his first feeding. Finally, he came back to himself and responded.

"I'm Nat. Nathaniel Bock. I'm...I'm a *vampire*? How...?" His voice trailed off. He was obviously in shock, not that I blamed him a bit.

"I found you very near death, Nathaniel. That you had not died before I found you is a miracle all by itself. Your will to survive is what made me decide to bring you over." I leaned toward him and gently kissed his cold forehead, hoping to reassure and calm him.

At that moment, Nat fell over on top of me, burying his face in my chest and holding tightly to me, sobbing as though his heart was broken. I wrapped my arms around him and petted him as he cried, patting his back and stroking his sleek hair rhythmically. I could not make out whatever words he was saying as he cried, but I knew that he was mourning his lost humanity, and that it was important that I allow him to do this while he could.

After what seemed an hour, but which indeed could have been a shorter or longer time than that, he finally stopped crying and pulled away from me, looking up into my eyes. I could see that his fangs had emerged and that he was very probably unaware of this fact. It created some odd kind of feeling within me that I had never before experienced and what happened next was almost as though it was from a dream, a bizarre dance that brought to mind some of the rituals you see animals engage in on television and in some magazines.

I could not now tell you why I did it, but I pulled my old cotton t-shirt off and wordlessly offered this starving vampire child my own throat. He stared at me for perhaps a full minute before he finally comprehended what I was allowing him to do to me. Then, with a piteous cry, he lurched forward, clumsily piercing my flesh with his virgin fangs and then began to drink from me.

He fed there for several minutes before I gently pushed him away, though I allowed him to lick at the wound he had created on the side of my neck. It seemed to be a necessary part of whatever was going on between us.

When he sat up again, I could see that some of the dark thick blood he had taken from me encircled the outside of his lips, with some running down his chin, much like the face of an infant who has just finished feeding will have milk smeared across it. After having fed, Nathaniel's eyes were uniformly black, with no whites showing, giving him an even more otherworldly appearance than just the fangs had given him.

I slowly and gently used my discarded t-shirt to wipe the blood from his face and pulled him back to my chest, holding him close and humming to him as I had after I had fed from him days before, waiting for him to die.

"I remember...I heard you," he mumbled, his face registering sudden shock and realization. "You were there with me while I was...dying."

"Yes. I found you when you were almost gone, Nathaniel. I did feed from you, but I thought you were about to die, and I was starving. Then, when you hung on so much longer, I decided to turn you," I admitted to him. "It truly felt to me as though you were not ready to go just yet."

He cried a bit more, but not as strongly as he had earlier. Perhaps this was something that vampires were supposed to do with their fledglings. It obviously had not happened between me and my own maker. Maybe this was why I had rejected Andreas so very strongly when I finally met him as a relative equal beside the stream. The initial bond had not been made at the right time, so I felt no draw to him. My own fledgling, on the other hand, brought out all those instincts I had not known I could have.

"Oh, dear God," he cried out once or twice, his head in his hands, and I found myself wanting to make all of that pain he felt go away. I continued to hold him, but strengthened my hold around him and eventually felt his stress slowly begin to ease.

It seemed as though his feeding from me had opened a preternatural doorway between Nathaniel and myself and I could now feel his sadness, his hunger and his terror at what he had become. I could only assume that he was also now tuned in to whatever I was feeling.

He must have sensed my own confusion, because his crying abruptly stopped and he looked up at me once more. I could feel his question.

"You are my first Child of Blood, Nathaniel. I know as much about what is going on here as you. We are going to have to learn about how all of this works, together." I tried to fill my thoughts and my tone with as much reassurance as I could muster.

"I am *so* hungry, Siofra" he all but wailed to me. I nodded my understanding. I could feel his growing hunger inside me like a gnawing worm, and knew I would need to take him soon to feed, but first we had to take care of something else.

"Let's get you cleaned up and dressed, Nat, and then we'll see about getting a little someone to eat."

Glossary:

Ádhamh: (*adjective* AY-thuhv) red, earth

Andreas: (*pronoun* Ahn-DRAY-ahs)

Bean sí (*pronoun Gaelic* Ban'SHEE) supernatural creature that often sends warnings of impending doom

Bigod (*pronoun* Bih'GAWD) English colonel

Bodhrán (*noun Gaelic* BO'rawn) Irish drum

Dearg (*noun Gaelic* Djareg) red

Éirí Amach 1641 *(Gaelic* Eye'Ree Amach*)* The Irish Rebellion of 1641

Leannán sí (*Gaelic* Lee Ah Nan Shee) a race of the faerie folk

Mathúin (*noun Gaelic* MAH hoon) Bear

Ó Sé (*Gaelic* Oh'Shay) Translates to grandson or descendant of Sé

Sí: (noun *Gaelic* shee) a race of the faerie folk

Siofra: (*noun Gaelic* Shee'fruh) Elf

Sumaire: (*noun Gaelic* Shoe MAH'ree) Vampire

Don't miss out!

Visit the website below and you can sign up to receive emails whenever Anna Rose publishes a new book. There's no charge and no obligation.

https://books2read.com/r/B-A-MFMF-XRTS

BOOKS 2 READ

Connecting independent readers to independent writers.

About the Author

Anna Rose is the author of the Tales of the Dragonguard (about dragons, of course!) and The Sumaire Web series of vampire novels.

She is currently working on KAL'S HEART, the third story in the Tales of the Dragonguard, that began with AYA'S DRAGON, and continues with SARA'S FIRE. which is now available in both e-book and softcover at Amazon, and in ebook format at iTunes, Barnes & Noble, and other fine merchants.

KAL'S HEART continues the story of the high-flying Dragonguard. Kal, the Aerie-born son of Dragonguard parents, is faced with a mystery that affects not only the whole of the Dragonguard, but his family as well. Together, he and his unusual dragon, Spirit, must use their unique abilities to find out who is causing trouble for the Dragonguard and to his family.

Her newest venture with her stories and novels is turning them into audiobooks for those folks who prefer listening to books, rather than reading them, for whatever reason.

Amongst her other writing, Anna writes vampires who like what they are and aren't looking for a rescue. Her vampires bite, drink and kill. No bottled or bagged blood for these vampires!

The first novel in the series, SIOFRA, was released in late January of 2012. The first novel was followed by FIACH FOLA and then DROCH FOLA. There is also a short story called FEASTA FOLA. Anna is also working on the fourth novel in the Sumaire Web series, COSAN FOLA, which she hopes to have completed by the end of 2018.

She lives in usually sunny Southern California.

Read more at www.sumaire.com.

www.ingramcontent.com/pod-product-compliance
Lightning Source LLC
Chambersburg PA
CBHW050949120626
46552CB00001B/452